The Essential Ranger Pack

- ✓ GPS unit
- ✓ Waterproof matches
- ✓ Pocketknife
- ✓ Beanie
- ✓ Torch
- ✓ Batteries
- ✓ Binoculars
- ✓ Camera
- ✓ Emergency transmitter
- ✓ Warm waterproof jacket
- ✓ Scarf
- ✓ Gloves
- ✓ Mobile phone
- ✓ Rope
- ✓ Spade

Other titles in the *Ranger in Danger* series

Diablo's Doom
Ranger in Danger – in Africa

Hernando's Labyrinth
Ranger in Danger – in South America

King Cobra's Curse
Ranger in Danger – in India

Rapscallion's Revenge
Ranger in Danger – in Australia

Takama's Tyranny
Ranger in Danger – in the Pacific

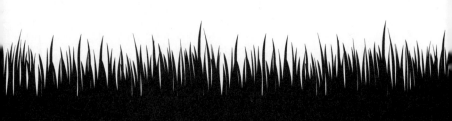

Erik's Enigma

Sean Willmore and Alison Reynolds

The Five Mile Press

For the 3 J's.
Janet Rowe for unleashing Ranger, Julia Taylor for taming it and
so much more, and Juliet Willcocks for setting it free.
AR

The Five Mile Press Pty Ltd
1 Centre Road, Scoresby
Victoria 3179 Australia
www.fivemile.com.au

Copyright © Sean Willmore and Alison Reynolds, 2010
All rights reserved

First published 2010

Cover and page design by Brad Maxwell
Illustrations by Andrew Hopgood
Typesetting by TypeSkill

National Library of Australia Cataloguing-in-Publication entry:

Willmore, Sean.
Erik's enigma / Sean Willmore & Alison Reynolds.
ISBN: 9781742480886 (pbk.)
Willmore, Sean. Ranger in danger; 5.
For primary school age.
Reynolds, Alison
A823.4

This book is printed and bound in Australia at McPherson's Printing Group.
The paper is manufactured from 100% recycled material.

It takes all
to create a whole world.

Rigmor Solem – Chief Ranger
Jotunheimen National Park, Norway

Scandinavia

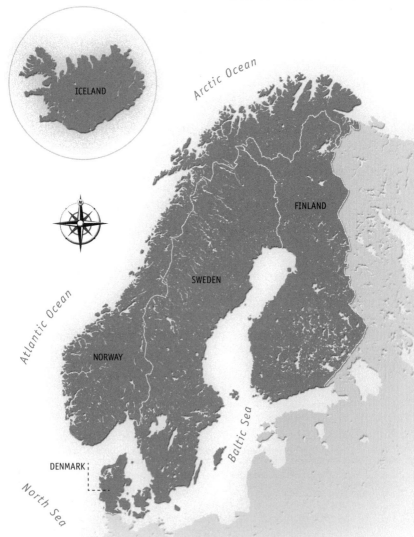

ICELAND

Arctic Ocean

FINLAND

SWEDEN

Atlantic Ocean

NORWAY

Baltic Sea

DENMARK

North Sea

To: Ranger in Danger
From: Rigmor Solem
Subject: Trouble

Want to visit Scandinavia? I could do with some help.
Hundreds of whales are beaching themselves on the
shores of some of our isolated national parks. I know this
occasionally happens in nature, but I've got a feeling
that something – or rather someone – is behind it.

I'll be honest: this is an extremely dangerous mission.
The last ranger we sent to investigate was discovered
frozen in a glacier, hundreds of kilometres away from
a national park. He had a Viking barbed spear, called a
krókspjót, impaled in his back. Experts authenticated the
age of the *krókspjót* as a hundred years old.

Are you prepared to risk certain danger? I'll understand
if you say no.

Best wishes,
Rigmor Solem

You've always wanted to visit Scandinavia – and whales!
You love whales and would do anything to help them
survive.
    But the main thing is that you can't let any more
rangers die in the line of duty. It's an easy choice.
    Quickly, you reply, 'YES.'
    Let the adventures begin!

Turn to page 2

Your boots crunch on the snow as you semi-jog after Rigmor, who speeds across the airport car park with her long strides. She stops at a red jeep covered in a light sprinkling of snow. 'It's a bit chilly,' she says, unlocking the car.

Is she joking? The temperature is subzero.

You jump into the jeep. Rigmor stands at the open driver's door and frowns at the sky. It's whitish with a tinge of yellow – a sign of snow.

'I need to find out if the airport has up-to-date information on weather and road conditions.' Rigmor breaks into a huge grin. 'Tonight we stay at an ice hotel.'

You smile and try to look overjoyed. You're sure it will be fun once you get there, but at the moment you're freezing and don't even want to think about ice.

You turn around to watch Rigmor lope towards the airport building. Something's written in the snow on the back window, but it must be in Scandinavian. You don't recognise any of the letters, but some of the symbols look like exclamation marks.

You crank up the heater and the melting snow forms a huge puddle around your boots. You glance in the mirror to check if Rigmor's on her way.

Suddenly, you can read the words written on the back window.

GO HOME RANGER IN DANGER!!!

Turn to page 3

From page 2

You leap out and rush around to the back of the jeep.
A jagged black stick lies in the snow. Whoever wrote
the warning must have chucked the stick there to avoid
being seen with it.

A trail of footprints in the snow stretches away
from the car park.

You take a deep breath. Your first response is to
follow the footprints, but Rigmor will be back in a second,
and maybe she should decide what you should do.

Something brushes against your cheek. You look up
and a snowflake scores a direct hit in your eye. *Ouch*.
You scrunch up your eyelid until the pain stops.

More and more snow floats down. Soon the
footprints will disappear and you could lose your only
chance to find out who wrote the message. Should you
wait for Rigmor? It's her territory and she's the expert
here.

If you decide to follow the footprints in the snow, turn to page 4
If you decide to wait for Rigmor, turn to page 13

More and more snowflakes float down, scattering the ground like icing sugar sifted over a cake. Soon there won't be a trail of footprints to follow.

You look across to the airport terminal. No sign of Rigmor. You can't wait any longer, you're off.

The footprints lead up a slope and towards a forest of Norwegian spruce. The snow clings to the dark green needle leaves. You feel like you're looking at hundreds of Christmas trees.

Inside, the forest is quiet. No bird calls, nothing. It's as if someone stuffed snow in your ears and blocked out all sound except for your panting breath.

The footprints wind between the trees, but you can't see or hear anybody. You don't like this. Maybe you should abandon the trail and return later with Rigmor. Probably whoever wrote the message fled long ago.

If you continue to follow the footprints, turn to page 6
If you decide to turn back, turn to page 117

From page 4

You shake yourself. This may be your one chance to find out who wrote the warning. You're not called the Ranger in Danger for nothing.

The footprints twist around and around. Whoever wrote the warning wasn't in a hurry, which seems weird.

Ahead you see a flash of red.

Quickly, you shelter behind a nearby tree to spy on the figure. He or she faces the other way from you, and wears a long red coat and a furry hat.

Your heart beats so loudly, the entire forest must hear it, but the red coat doesn't move a millimetre.

You slide your regulation ranger rope out of your pocket and charge towards the red-coated figure. With a yell, you fling the rope over the head and pull tight around the waist.

The figure crumples and topples over. The fur hat falls off to reveal a crushed snowball. You just attacked a snowman.

Your face turns as red as the snowman's coat. It's lucky no-one was around to see that.

A loud clapping sound fills the forest.

Turn to page 7

A tall man with long sandy hair and a neatly trimmed beard emerges from the trees. He looks like a Viking, in a cape made from reindeer fur and a metal helmet with two horns. He also holds an eighty-centimetre-long sword in his fur-gloved hands.

Oh boy!

'Some of my business colleagues warned me that you were a nosy creature.' He strides easily towards you in snow shoes that distribute his weight evenly across the snow. He doesn't sink with each step like you do in your boots.

'I would bid you welcome to Norway, but you're not welcome at all.'

He swings his sword back and forth slowly, squeezing the simple metal cross handle.

You need to think fast. He has a sword and you have a pocketknife. You could sprint away, but that won't be easy in the forest through the snow. Also, you're not even sure which way to run.

He steps forward.

If you try to run away, turn to page 75
If you stay, turn to page 8

From page 7

Desperately, you scan the forest. There must be a way to get out of this alive.

'Allow me to introduce myself,' says the man. 'I'm Erik, a modern-day Viking.'

'A modern-day phoney, if you ask me.' You sound calm, but really you want to curl up in a ball and scream.

'Prepare to die!' shouts Erik, raising his sword.

Something moves in the conifer above Erik's head. You quickly examine the tree and observe the large brownish-black head and small ears of a male wolverine. A male wolverine looks a bit like a bear, but it's the largest land-dwelling species of the weasel family.

Your head swirls with the many facts you know about wolverines. Two specific facts stick out. One: the wolverine is an opportunistic hunter and it ambushes its prey, sometimes by jumping down on it from above. Two: it's very short-sighted. Wolverines don't attack humans, but if you can get Erik to bend over, then maybe, with his fur cloak and two horns sticking out of his head, he might look like some sort of strange animal.

'I give up!' you shout and throw your pocketknife down on the snow.

Erik leans down to scoop it up. 'Sorry, little ranger, but you still have to exit ... Agghhhh!'

Turn to page 10

Bullseye!

The wolverine straddles Erik's back, but you don't wait to see what happens next.

You run screaming through the forest. Twigs and leaves from overhanging branches hit and poke your eyes, your ears, your hair, but you don't stop. You need to get as far away from Erik as possible. You wonder who will be angrier, Erik or the wolverine? You don't want to meet Erik after eighteen kilograms of angry, hungry, clawing wolverine has pounced on his back.

Shouts ring out, but you sprint onwards. You won't feel safe until you're locked up safely in the ranger jeep with the engine roaring.

A hand grabs your jacket.

Turn to page 11

'Halt!' Rigmor yells in your ear. 'It's me.'

You collapse in the snow and struggle to catch your breath. 'A Viking ... a Viking nearly killed me,' you say.

Rigmor stares at you with her mouth wide open.

'He had horns, and a sword,' you say. 'He's a Viking.'

'Did you bump your head?' Her voice is concerned. 'The true Vikings wore a helmet without horns. The image of a Viking wearing horns arose in the late nineteenth century to attract bigger audiences to operas.'

'His name was Erik. Erik the Viking.'

Rigmor's mouth forms a straight line. 'Erik's an enemy to the environment and to all rangers. He's ruthless. He runs a huge international mining company that bends every rule. Its mining activities cause untold damage to the natural world. Yet he claims descent from the Vikings. The Vikings looked after the environment.'

'Well, he's not a very happy Viking just now.' You explain about Erik and a certain male wolverine.

Tears run down Rigmor's cheeks as she laughs and laughs. 'This is very good news, indeed. At last we have a reliable witness to testify against him – he can be charged with attempted murder.'

'But he'll escape,' you say, slowly. 'I should have tried to disarm him.'

Sometimes you're a total loser as a ranger.

Turn to page 12

11

Rigmor smiles. 'Do you remember what male wolverines often do with their prey?' she asks.

Suddenly, you feel much better. 'They spray their prey with scent gland secretions to stop other animals from eating it. The scent is similar to a skunk's.'

'Exactly. So if we get road-blocks set up in the immediate vicinity, all we'll need to do is to ask the police to sniff for a human stink bomb, and Erik will be off for a long stint in jail.'

You grin. 'Don't you mean a long stink in jail!'

THE END

From page 3

You stop yourself from following the footprints and, instead, watch the snowflakes cover the ground.

'Why aren't you in the car?' Rigmor strides towards you.

You point to the back window.

'Go home ranger in danger,' she reads aloud.

She bites her bottom lip and frowns. 'I do not know if I have the right to expect you to help.'

'It's my decision,' you say, 'and I want to be here.'

'I hope you never regret your choice,' she murmurs.

'Shall we follow the footprints, while we can?' she asks.

Rigmor glides across the car park and up the slope towards a forest of huge Norwegian spruce trees. You trudge next to her, feeling like a clumsy, waddling duck.

13

Turn to page 14

From page 13

Inside the forest, the footprints are easy to trace because the tall conifers protect the ground from the falling snow.

'Come on!' you shout as you follow the trail into a wide gap between two trees.

You slap your hand over your mouth. You're meant to be conducting surveillance, and one of the ranger rules is to do it quietly. Everyone within a kilometre vicinity probably heard you.

Rigmor yells, 'Stop!'

Ahead, you hear a crackle as if someone is lurking nearby and has brushed against the lower branches of a tree.

'Wait!' screams Rigmor.

If you head towards the crackling sound, turn to page 15
If you listen to Rigmor, turn to page 18

14

This could be your only chance to catch the lurker, that's if Rigmor quietens down and doesn't scare away whoever it is. She must not be able to hear the sound of someone close by. Luckily, you are a trained observer.

'I'll be back,' you whisper as you run ahead across the smooth snow.

'Aggghhh!' you scream as you fall through snow and twigs and moss to land with a crunch in a pit.

You try to pull yourself into a sitting position. Pain shoots up your leg. Somehow, your foot points the wrong way. You flop backwards.

Your fingers close around something. It feels like a large ring.

Rigmor peers down.

Her face shimmers in front of you, then everything fades to black.

15

Turn to page 16

Someone groans loudly. You're about to tell them to keep quiet, but you realise that it's you. You open your eyes and see that your foot is hoisted high in the air. Snowy white plaster covers your leg from toes to knee.

You tell yourself, 'Great effort, ranger!' Your adventures in Scandinavia are over. Tears well up in your eyes and your nose runs. You can't be bothered searching for tissues so you have a huge sniff.

'You're awake,' says Rigmor's voice.

You jump. So much for being a trained observer. You don't know when someone's a metre away from you, let alone when you risk falling into a pit.

'I should have listened to you, Rigmor.' You twist around to face her in the chair beside your bed. 'I wrecked everything.'

She grins. 'All isn't lost. Someone wanted us to follow the footprints, and he or she dug a reindeer trap, but this time it was a ranger trap. Reindeer traps haven't been used since the 1800s. This trap was perfectly constructed: two metres deep, two metres long and just over half a metre wide. It was covered with twigs and moss, then the falling snow disguised it further.'

'But you saw it,' you say.

'Only because this is my land, and I've seen old reindeer traps. The slightly raised rectangle of snow made me immediately suspicious.'

Turn to page 17

Rigmor frowns. 'You fell in, just like a reindeer that is trapped until the hunters return and kill it.'

'I should be called Ranger who *is* a Danger.'

'Don't say that. Do you remember picking up this in the pit?' She holds out a small, decorated bone ring, that's four centimetres in diameter. Carvings of harts, male deer, decorate it.

'Yes, vaguely. What is it? you ask.

'It's an ancient thumb ring used by archers to protect their thumbs as they drew their bows, which weighed more than forty-five kilograms. To fire the arrow, the archer hooked the string around his thumb, so the string rested on the ring.'

You shrug. 'So someone left a thumb ring in the trap over one hundred years ago.'

17

'The ranger trap was just built. The ring was left by someone today,' says Rigmor. 'It's a unique, well-documented and recently bought thumb ring.'

You smile slowly. 'So he left his calling card.'

Rigmor laughs. 'He's in jail for causing bodily harm. It's safer now to be a ranger with him behind bars.'

Rigmor writes with a marker on your plaster:
'DON'T GO HOME RANGER! WE NEED YOU.'

THE END

From page 14

You turn to hush Rigmor, but stop when you see that she looks dead-white.

'Back away carefully,' Rigmor orders.

You stare at the smooth expanse of snow in front of you. You observe how a large rectangle about two metres long and just over half a metre wide, is slightly higher than the surrounding ground.

Carefully, you retreat and rejoin Rigmor. She breaks off a long twig from a fir tree and creeps up to the raised rectangle.

She thrusts the stick into the snow. Nothing happens.

You lean down and quickly gather snow together to form a ball. The snow is so cold it burns your bare hands and your fingers become numb, but you don't stop until you make a giant snowball.

It's too heavy to lift by yourself. 'Want to help, Rigmor?' you ask.

'Excellent idea,' she says with a grin.

The two of you heave up the snow ball and toss it onto the snowy rectangle.

You hear a crack and the ball disappears into the ground, right where you were about to step before Rigmor called you back.

Turn to page 20

From page 18

Rigmor stops grinning as she peers into a pit. 'A reindeer trap. But no normal reindeer trap was ever lined with sticks like these.'

Sharp sticks line the bottom of the hole. You shiver at your narrow escape from being skewered. If you hadn't listened to Rigmor's warning, or if you had decided to follow the footprints by yourself then ... 'Thanks,' you murmur. 'Someone planned for us to fall in this ... this ranger trap.'

'You're right, it is a ranger trap,' says Rigmor, frowning. 'No-one makes reindeer traps now, not since the 1800s. I know this forest and this trap wasn't here yesterday. But whoever made it is extremely skilful, because it's very hard to see.'

'I never noticed it,' you admit.

Turn to page 21

From page 20

Rigmor says, 'I only observed it because I've seen them before. It's a standard-size reindeer trap: two metres deep, two metres long and just over half a metre wide. Someone covered it with twigs and moss, then the falling snow disguised it further.'

You stare down at the sharp sticks and shiver.

'What do you want to do?' asks Rigmor. 'Maybe you should heed the warning and return home. Our enemy is both smart and ruthless. He or she guessed we would follow the footprints.'

Back at home, you would be warm. No standing in a forest with numb hands and, hopefully, no-one trying to kill you.

Rigmor watches you and waits for your decision.

Suddenly, an explosion shakes the ground.

You and Rigmor charge out of the forest towards the car park. Black smoke billows into the air and orange, red and yellow flames burn fiercely.

'It looks as if I need a new jeep,' says Rigmor in a quiet voice.

Turn to page 22

Five hours later, you and Rigmor are winding around hairpin bends as you head for the ice lodge situated in a national park. Towering larch trees and huge boulders dusted in snow line the roadsides, and the borrowed jeep slowly climbs up the mountain.

Rigmor looks serious as she grips the steering wheel. 'Twice we face attempts to scare us away. I hope there is no third attempt.'

Honk! Rigmor bangs a fist on the horn and slams her foot on the brake as a 300 kilogram musk ox with sharp, curved horns saunters onto the narrow road. It's massive, with a deep brown coat, lighter patches on its nose, and a slight hump behind its shoulders.

Its long, shaggy hair that must be more than sixty centimetres long, nearly sweeps the road. The musk ox has the longest hair of any animal in the world, except humans. It can withstand incredibly cold temperatures as low as minus fifty degrees celsius, due to its thick wool, which is the world's most valuable and warmest.

Rigmor honks the horn again. The musk ox starts, then paws the ground and snorts.

It would be so good to have a photo for your Ranger in Danger collection. Musk oxen have existed for more than 20,000 years. They're prehistoric.

You pull out your camera from your backpack.

Rigmor glances across at you, 'Maybe don't ...'

If you take a photo, turn to page 23
If you don't take a photo, turn to page 36

Too late. Your camera flashes, lighting up the roadway.

The musk ox seems to glare at the jeep. She doesn't look pleased.

You ask, 'Rigmor, isn't the musk ox normally a passive animal in its contact with humans?'

'Yes,' Rigmor says.

You wish her voice sounded more certain.

The musk ox snorts as loudly as a jackhammer.

Next moment, 300 kilograms of fury hurtles towards the car.

Rigmor yanks the gear stick into reverse, and slams her foot down on the accelerator. The jeep jumps backwards and Rigmor reverses down the road.

She manages to reverse around the first two corners like a race car driver, and relief oozes through you. 'The only human fatality caused by a musk ox in Norway was when someone took a photo,' she mutters, as she concentrates on the road behind you.

The next corner is a hairpin bend, and the musk ox shows no sign of slowing. You wish you didn't know that musk oxen are capable of running sixty kilometres per hour.

You glimpse something zooming up behind you.

'Watch out,' you scream. 'A truck!'

Turn to page 24

Rigmor swerves onto the other side of the road. The truck thunders past and the musk ox charges into the forest, but the jeep spins around and its two right-hand tyres hit the gravel.

The jeep spins off the road, down the side of the mountain.

It slides into a huge boulder and stops with a shudder. The bonnet crumples up, and the radio pops out and smashes on the floor.

Shocked, you stare down the steep cliff outside your window, and you want to vomit, cry and go to the toilet all at once. You nearly fell off the side of the mountain. You'll never forgive yourself if Rigmor is hurt because of your stupid photo.

'Rigmor?' you say in a soft voice. The jeep tips forwards at a forty-five degree angle, which makes it hard to turn around and look beside you.

Rigmor slumps in her seat with her eyes shut. Her entire body shakes. You try again. 'Rigmor, where are you hurt? I'm sorry.'

'I'm fine,' she says, wiping her eyes.

You realise she's laughing, not crying. That can be a typical reaction to shock. You need to reassure her.

Turn to page 25

'Rigmor, we nearly died. If you had swerved another metre we wouldn't be here. Only this boulder protects us from certain death. But we're okay.'

She smiles. 'I'm laughing because I can't believe I wrecked two cars in one day. What will the other rangers say?'

You grin. You're sure they'll have plenty to say once you meet them. 'I'll ring them on my mobile phone.' You pat your pocket, but then you remember that you lost your phone in the car explosion at the airport.

Rigmor's fingers tightly clench the steering wheel. 'My phone, too, was blown-up.'

Fear washes over you, but you try to shrug it away. 'Can you climb though the window?' you ask.

Rigmor unclips her seatbelt. The jeep moves slightly.

'The ground is very unstable with this powdery snow,' she says with a frown.

'But no-one will find us here,' you reply. 'We spun way down the side of the mountain.'

'Should we stay here or leave?' asks Rigmor.

'Let's go,' you announce and jump out of the jeep.

25

Turn to page 26

You land with a crash on the thin layer of ice covering the snow.

'Wait!' shouts Rigmor.

'Hurry up, Rigmor.' You jump up and down to warm up.

You hear an ominous cracking noise.

'Keep still!' screams Rigmor.

You thunk down on your bottom. All around you, the ice shatters and gravity seems to suck the snow down the mountain. A loud noise like a steam train fills your ears, but you're nowhere near a railway.

The snow sweeps you away. Firs flash past and you travel so fast you're breathless.

It's an avalanche!

Turn to page 28

From page 26

It's like being in a giant snow waterfall as you tumble down the mountain. Urgently, you grab at a passing tree. Your hand closes around a branch. The snow pushes you, but you hold on tightly. You know an avalanche travels 100 to 130 kilometres per hour.

If you can hold onto this branch, you'll be out of the main path of the avalanche and your chances of survival will improve incredibly. Ice and snow showers you, and you grip the branch tighter and tighter.

Suddenly, the branch snaps and you roll down the mountain, clutching a useless long twig – in what feels like a giant washing-machine full of snow and ice. You tumble over and over. Snow is everywhere. In your boots, your underwear, even under your eyelids. You choke as snow rams into your mouth every time you gasp for a breath.

You need to think fast to have any chance of survival. What do you do in an avalanche?

If you keep your body straight with your arms by your side, turn to page 135

If you make swimming motions with your body, turn to page 29

28

From page 28

You need to forget that hundreds of tonnes of snow and ice threaten to smother you. You know that lying still in an avalanche is the worst thing to do.

You try to remain on the surface of the slide, and you make swimming motions with your arms and legs, interspersed with star-jump motions. Your muscles scream in pain as you fight against the snow and gravity to stop being pulled under.

Slowly, the snow sucks you down, but you don't stop fighting. Finally, the avalanche starts to slow. If only you had a safety beacon. Hold on, you still clutch the long twig. You thrust it up and hope part of it remains visible above the surface.

Next, you punch your hands out in front of your face to create an air pocket. When the avalanche stops, the snow will soon harden.

You want to scream and shout, but you force yourself to breathe slowly. The oxygen in the air pocket is limited, and if you shout and breathe rapidly you'll use up too much oxygen and suffocate.

It's useless to shout anyway, unless Rigmor is close-by. Snow muffles sound. All you can do is wait and hope.

Turn to page 30

Minutes pass. You know that ninety-three per cent of avalanche victims survive if dug out within fifteen minutes. After that time, fatalities skyrocket.

You wish Rigmor would hurry up.

The snow hardens and soon you feel as if plaster encases your entire body. This is your own fault. In ninety per cent of avalanche incidents, the victim or someone else in their group triggered the avalanche. When you jumped on the snow, you must have caused huge sheets of snow to fracture like shattered glass, and then all the sheets slid off the mountain together as a unit, causing an avalanche.

Rigmor realised what was going to happen and that's why she shouted for you to stop.

If she's going to dig you out in time, she needs to find you now!

'*Rigmor!!!!!!*' you scream.

Turn to page 31

Stop panicking, you tell yourself. Hopefully, Rigmor maintained visual contact of you and took some sort of visual cue of where she last saw you. This will mark the upper boundary of her search area.

The ranger jeep will have a shovel, especially in a snowy country like Norway. Rigmor will need to pick her way carefully over the slide zone to avoid triggering another avalanche, but she should be here by now. Where is she?

Your head aches. It might be the first sign of hypercapnia, which is carbon dioxide poisoning. Soon you'll be short of breath and delirious, and then you'll die.

Bang! Then you hear a scraping noise.

It's somewhere just near your head.

Rigmor! She's found you. Once you locate the victim, you dig downhill of the site until you expose the head and chest.

Turn to page 32

The snow falls away slowly, and you gaze up at Rigmor's smiling, bright red face.

'I feared you were lost,' she puffs, as she continues to shovel. 'I glimpsed the end of the stick jutting up through the snow. You've been under for four minutes.'

Four minutes! 'It felt like four years,' you say.

She helps you up, and you dust off the snow.

You feel surprisingly well. Nothing broken or even bruised. 'I'll never be able to thank you enough, Rigmor.'

'We are both rangers. You are my family,' says Rigmor with a shrug. She steps forward and winces.

'You're injured,' you say.

'I turned my ankle a little while I was searching for you. It is nothing.' She stares at the vast plain of snow in front of you and sighs. 'What are you like at hiking through snow?'

You kneel down and gently touch her ankle.

She screams.

'I'm going to give you first aid, then hike until I find help. You'll be safe if I make you an ice cave to shelter in.'

'It's too dangerous. We'll stay here.' She takes a step, then bites her lips so hard to stop from crying out, that you see a drop of blood.

Turn to page 33

From page 32

First things first. You help Rigmor hop to a fallen log. It's getting dark, so you need to build a snow shelter. Snow and ice are freezing cold, but they are also excellent insulators.

You grab Rigmor's shovel, trudge over to the nearby fir plantation and select a tall, sturdy-looking tree. You dig beside it into the snow and soon you've made a tunnel big enough for you and Rigmor.

You make sure the top of the shelter is one-and-a-bit metres below the upper surface of the snow. You find a long stick and poke that up to the surface to make a ventilation hole, so you and Rigmor won't suffocate.

Rigmor moans. You race to collect fir boughs and bark, which you place on the bottom of the shelter. This means you won't lie directly on the snow and lose body heat.

'Finished.' You crawl out of the shelter.

You kneel in front of Rigmor and apply basic first aid to her ankle. At least there's plenty of snow available to make an icepack. You bandage the joint firmly with your scarf and help her into the shelter. You pile up a small stack of branches for her to place her foot on to raise it higher than her heart and help reduce swelling.

'Done,' you announce.

She smiles and flops back on the fir branches. She looks so ill, you're scared.

If you decide to go for help, turn to page 69
If you decide to stay where you are, turn to page 34

From page 33

One part of you wants to run and find help for Rigmor. If only you had listened to her and not jumped out of the jeep. Then there would have been no avalanche, and Rigmor wouldn't be here trying not to cry because her ankle hurts so much. Everything is your fault.

You lie beside Rigmor and talk quietly to her about your adventures. You know basic ranger rules. Stay where you are until you get rescued. Rigmor drifts off, but whenever you stop talking she stirs. You talk and talk until you're hoarse.

It's actually surprisingly warm inside the ice shelter. Every hour, you poke a stick up the ventilation hole to stop it becoming blocked by snow.

34

Eventually, it's morning. You crawl out of the shelter and an elk saunters through the fir trees. It's huge – about 2.3 metres high. The elk's antlers will grow to more than two metres by the end of summer, but now they're covered with a soft, fuzzy skin called velvet, as they begin to grow. The elk stalks up to a fir tree and strips off the bark. Elks can't bite in a snipping motion, because they only have a bottom set of teeth.

'What's happening out there?' calls Rigmor.

The elk hurdles easily over a large log and disappears. Its front legs are longer than its rear legs, which makes it easier to jump over fallen trees in the forest.

'I'm about to start Operation Our Rescue,' you say.

Turn to page 35

You've made a sign out of rocks and sticks: *S.O.S.*

'Will this do?' you ask.

'It's an excellent job.' Rigmor sits on a log.

You smile.

'And I had a surprisingly good sleep last night. All thanks to you.'

You stare down at her ankle. 'But I ruined everything. We still need to find out so much. For a start, who wanted me to leave Norway?'

Rigmor looks serious. 'Alas, our enemy will not disappear. He or she will wait. Perhaps it is better if we move more slowly. Our enemy will wonder what to expect.'

'So in the meantime, we wait for our rescue?'

A flock of ravens fly overhead.

'We may be rescued soon. People call a flock of ravens an "unkindness". But a raven led to the discovery of Iceland. A Norwegian Viking called Floki set sail with three ravens to search for a new land. He released one raven. It returned to Norway. Then he released the second raven, which flew around and returned to the ship exhausted. He released the third raven, which flew forwards. Floki followed it and discovered a new land, Iceland.'

You and Rigmor watch in silence as a helicopter appears over the mountains.

THE END

35

From page 22

You place your camera back on your lap.

Rigmor smiles at you. 'Thanks. I've only heard of one death caused by a musk ox in Norway. It was a man who snapped a photo.'

You gulp. 'I thought the musk ox was passive and shy towards humans. I know it's vegetarian and lives on lichen, herbs, larch trees and other things.'

'I don't fear being eaten,' says Rigmor. 'I'm more worried about being squashed. This musk ox is a big girl. When a wolf attacks a musk ox and bites its stomach, the musk ox merely rolls over, and squashes and kills the wolf.'

The musk ox bellows, sounding like a lion. You and Rigmor both jump. A baby musk ox wanders onto the road. It's a perfect smaller replica of its mother, but without horns.

Turn to page 38

From page 36

'So that's why the musk ox is so upset,' says Rigmor. 'They're extremely protective mothers. I suppose that's how the species survived the Ice Age, while all the woolly mammoths perished.'

Eight other musk oxen march onto the road and form a circle around the baby, with their horns facing outwards. You're heard this is typical defensive behaviour. Slowly, they shepherd the baby back into the forest.

'When a musk ox is killed, the herd tries to surround the body to prevent it from being eaten,' says Rigmor. 'Unfortunately, this defensive behaviour makes it all too easy for a hunter to kill off the entire herd. Sometimes a human hunter claims he or she cannot collect the killed animal without shooting the protective animals. As rangers, it is our duty to educate people, and make them realise the huge impact of massacring an entire herd.'

She turns the ignition. Soon, you're over the other side of the mountain and you look down into the valley.

You gasp.

Turn to page 40

Amongst the winter skeletons of birches and larches, a huge, pink, cathedral-like structure gleams like a jewel. Every year, the owners build it in a different design. Nearby, you glimpse a white waterfall surging down a sheer cliff.

'Welcome to the ice hotel,' announces Rigmor.

It's unbelievable, but you feel warmer inside the ice hotel because of the insulating properties of the ice. The hotel's temperature varies between minus four and minus five degrees Celsius, depending on the number of guests and the outside temperatures. Every winter, steel pillars are positioned and thousands of tonnes of snow are moulded around these pillars using snow cannons and front-end loaders. The snow 'sets' after eight hours, and the pillars are removed. This must be one of the most fun jobs in the world.

Later, you leave your bedroom rugged up in the fake fur coat, hat and gloves, which the hotel provides for all its guests. Tonight you'll sleep in a thermal sleeping bag on a special bed made of ice and covered with reindeer skins.

You stare at the glowing ice wall of the long hallway. A sign warns, 'Do not lick.'

You look up and down the hall. No-one's around.

If you lick the wall, turn to page 41
If you don't lick the wall, turn to page 56

Surely you can get away with a quick lick. You can be speedy. How can you resist disobeying the sign?

You check nobody's coming. Voices flow out of a room, but you'll be too fast for anyone to catch you.

The ice wall is shiny and so white that it glows. Your breath puffs out in small white clouds. You breathe on the wall to warm it up, even though it would take more than your puny breath to do that. A slight sheen of moisture appears.

Quickly, you dart out the tip of your tongue.

Agggghhhh! The ice grips your flesh like superglue. The voices in the nearby room become louder; the people must be leaving.

This is embarrassing.

You tune in on the voices. It's two men.

'Need to ... rid of them,' murmurs a soft voice.

'Stupid whales, serves them right,' rumbles a loud, deep voice.

What? You shut your eyes and concentrate so that you don't miss a word.

The soft voice talks again. 'They'll snoop around.'

'Nothing stops my mining operations. Thor's thunder, man! You know what to do. Kill the rangers!' roars the deep voice.

41

Turn to page 42

You swallow hard, which is extremely difficult when your tongue is stuck to an ice wall. You need to get out of here, and warn Rigmor.

Experimentally, you tug your tongue. No movement at all.

The two men talk softly again, but you can't catch their words. They must have moved away from the door. With a bit of luck they are discussing who sleeps in which bed and they'll stay in the bedroom the whole night.

You hear a cough. The deep voiced man says, 'Let's go.'

You look sideways and see a tall man with shoulder length hair and a neatly trimmed beard emerge into the hallway.

'What have we here?' he asks in his deep voice, pushing his hair behind his ears. 'Look at this!'

Another man rushes out. He's short with blond hair. 'Erik, I'll take care of this young person, who must be a ranger.' He strides towards you. 'The rangers are the only other people booked on this floor. I made sure of that.'

Oh boy. Here you are with your tongue stuck to a wall, and you definitely don't like it when the blond guy pulls a long hunting knife out of his coat pocket as he nears you.

Turn to page 44

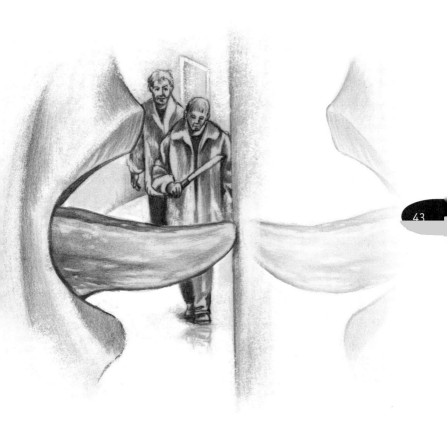

43

The blond-haired guy is mere metres away. You have no choice. You brace yourself and rip your tongue off the wall. You squeak from the excruciating pain. You feel as if half your tongue's left on the ice, but you can't worry about that now. You need to get out of here fast.

At the end of the hall, you see a window. You charge towards it, and leap onto the ice windowsill. The air is much colder outside than inside the hotel, but your fake fur coat, hat and gloves should keep you warm.

You stare down at the snow, which is lit up by the hotel lights. It's a big drop, but you have no choice. It's now or never.

You soar from the window, but your body stops with a jolt. Instead of falling to the ground, you dangle in mid-air.

You twist your head around and see the blond man's knife implanted in the hem of your fur coat, pinning it to the windowsill. You're not going anywhere.

The tall, bearded man grins down at you. 'Thor's thunder, what have we here? A very odd prey you've caught me this time, Lars.'

Turn to page 45

You feel like a wriggling salmon in a net, but no way will you let these men have the satisfaction of seeing you scared. Instead, you pull off a glove and dab your tongue with your finger, as if it's just a slight inconvenience that you're dangling in space.

'I'm Erik, the true descendant of the Vikings,' announces the tall man.

He waits expectantly, but you stare intently at your finger where you observe a minuscule smear of blood from your tongue.

'Oh, brave ranger,' mocks Erik, 'so soon to follow your former ranger colleague into a glacier. Until we capture the famous Rigmor Solem, we'll need to put you on ice, but that presents no problems around here.'

He waves his arm at all the snow and ice, and Lars guffaws appreciatively. You pretend to yawn, and pull your glove back on.

'Bored, are you? You interfering rangers will poke your noses into my mining operations. All because of those stupid whales. Everyone says they're so intelligent, but if they're so intelligent why can't they tell the difference between the sonar waves of a submarine and the sonar waves of a whale? Stupid fish.'

Turn to page 46

'They're actually mammals, not fish,' you say. 'And that explains why so many of them are beaching themselves. It's your fault. Why are you even *in* national park waters?'

'I told you, I'm a Viking. The seas belong to me. I requested to do a little exploratory investigation for my mining company, but your lot refused me. What's a Viking meant to do?' smirks Erik. 'So I started running cultural tours on my Viking longship. No-one seems to have realised that they're permanently booked up, and no tourist has ever set foot on the ship.'

Lars laughs heartily.

'You can't get away with this,' you say. 'Anyway, you're not a real Viking warrior because you have a beard. Real Vikings didn't grow beards so that their opponents couldn't grab them during fights.'

Erik frowns. 'I'm beginning to find you very boring. I'm going now, because I have many things to do. Lars, get rid of this little ranger.' He disappears.

Lars grins and starts to haul you up by the fake fur coat.

That's it! Your fur coat! Quickly you wriggle out of it and crash to the ground.

If you run straight back to the hotel entrance, turn to page 54
If you run away from the hotel, turn to page 47

From page 46

You roll over in the snow, then jump up and dash into the nearby woods. Your heart thuds as you charge between the fir trees. You lean on a trunk for a second to get your breath back, and grab your pocketknife from inside your shirt.

Lars hurtles out of the window and collapses in the snow like a bag of turnips. A second later, he staggers up and trudges over to meet Erik, who saunters out through the front door.

It's lucky you decided to run into the woods rather than back to the hotel entrance. You feel even luckier when you see Erik draw a long sword from under his fur coat. He and Lars track your path easily by your footprints in the snow and rush towards the woods.

You need to concentrate. Somehow you need to return to the hotel and tell Rigmor about Erik, his mining company and the whales. You can't run around the woods indefinitely.

Your chances are probably better near the hotel. Rigmor should search for you soon. You study the hotel. Lars has returned and stands guard in front of it. And Erik ... Where is he? Great work ranger, you tell yourself, you've lost him. He could creep up on you at any moment.

Turn to page 48

Erik has a sword. You have a pocketknife. Presumably he knows the area, and you've never been here before.

You could yell out for help, but that would alert Erik and Lars to where you are.

You stare at the ice hotel which glows with orange lights as night arrives. It's amazing to think that once spring arrives the hotel will melt and the water will be absorbed back into the river that winds through the property.

You wait for Erik with every nerve alert in your body. The muscles in your legs twitch in readiness to flee.

He's coming. You hear something moving close by.

A loud snort breaks the silence. Unless Erik has a terrible cold, this must be an animal. You risk flicking on your ranger torch.

A huge reindeer pads towards you. The rims of its hooves cut into the icy snow and stop it from slipping. The reindeer is a male bull that must weigh over 300 kilograms, with antlers that are over one hundred centimetres wide. It's magnificent.

The reindeer crumples to the ground as you hear a small, popping sound. Blood spreads over the snow.

Turn to page 50

From page 48

'There you are.' Erik slinks out quietly from behind the trees like an Eurasian lynx. 'I couldn't resist killing Bambi; such a huge specimen. Lars can fetch him later. Lucky, I had my pistol with the silencer so no-one in the hotel will decide to cramp my style by investigating. For you, I have a special treat.'

He holds his sword out in front of him. 'You might be interested in this sword, young ranger. It's a 900-year-old Viking sword. The Vikings made their swords from iron, with a sharp point for thrusting.'

He jabs it towards you and laughs. 'Note, too, that both sides of the sword are sharp. It's called a double-edged sword, and both sides of the blade can cut and slice.' He slowly raises his sword.

Hastily, you throw your pocketknife at his bare hand. He winces, but you don't wait to check out his injury. You gallop towards the sheds at the side of the hotel near the river.

50

Turn to page 51

Various equipment stands outside the sheds: a front-
end loader; something that looks like a cannon; and a
snowmobile.

You leap into the snowmobile, and pull down the
lever to start it. Nothing.

You try again.

Erik emerges from the woods and gestures for Lars
to join him. They head towards the sheds.

One last try. The snowmobile stays cold and useless.
You spot a battery shoved behind your seat. That's the
problem.

Erik and Lars stride towards you. They'll reach you
in seconds.

51

If you give up and look for another plan, turn to page 52
If you try and connect the battery, turn to page 111

You pick up the battery, but drop it when you see how close Erik and Lars are. You don't have time to try to connect it.

Somewhere, there must be something to help you.

You gaze at the cannon. It's the snow cannon that was used to construct the ice hotel.

You leap out of the snowmobile, grab a huge bucket, and you run to the river and back.

'What's he doing?' ask Lars.

They're so close that you wait for Erik to pierce you with his sword.

You flick on the snow cannon and snow spurts out, showering Erik and Lars.

They yell and try to flee, but you keep a steady spray of snow on them.

Turn to page 53

From page 52

Erik drops his sword, and falls to the ground.

You scream for help, and Rigmor and the hotel staff run out.

Rigmor stares at the frosty figures of Erik and Lars. 'What happened?'

'I've found out what – or rather who – caused the whales to beach. It's Erik the self-styled Viking. He was conducting illegal explorations for his mining company, using a submarine in the national park waters.'

'Confusing the sonar detectors of the poor whales,' finishes Rigmor. 'But why the sword?'

'He claims to be a Viking.'

Rigmor sniffs. 'He is no Viking. They respected nature. They only fished and hunted as much as they needed. They would never plunder the land for their own greed. They knew their destiny was entwined with the health of the environment.'

'Where will we put them to defrost?' asks one of the staff.

'In the sauna,' says Rigmor.

The staff shuffles Erik and Lars past you. Lars shivers uncontrollably, while Erik looks as if he would snarl, but his face is too frozen to move.

'Enjoy the warmth, Erik and Lars,' you say, 'because soon you'll be in the cooler for a very long time.'

THE END

From page 46

You roll over in the snow, and leap to your feet.

The hotel entrance is only fifty metres away. You charge towards it, your boots ploughing through the snow.

You hear a loud thud and glance over your shoulder. Lars has followed you through the window. He staggers to his feet in the snow, and chases you.

You've always been an excellent sprinter, and although the snow slows you down, it slows Lars down even more. You'll make it to the entrance first. Rigmor will be interested to find the real reason for the beached whales. It's all Erik's fault.

The door to the Ice Hotel is shut. Deafening music suddenly pumps out.

You grab the reindeer antler front door handle and twist it.

The door swings open slowly and you race in.

Turn to page 55

'Good evening,' says Erik, with a wide grin.

'How ...?' you stammer.

'Little ranger, a good hunter always has a back-up plan. You fell right into my trap. I told you I was going; I just failed to say that I was going to the front door in case you had any ideas of coming back here to try to save Rigmor.'

You swing around, but Lars has finally caught up and guards the door.

'Help!' you scream over the *boomph boomph* of the music.

'Unfortunately for you, no-one will hear you. I took the precaution of dropping off a CD to the others, who are all in the kitchen. I said it needed to be played loud.'

Desperately, you pull out your pocketknife.

Erik gazes at it, thoughtfully. 'It's a fine piece of workmanship, but unfortunately no match for the type of knife I prefer to use.'

He pulls out a gleaming gold sword from inside his coat.

THE END

'Don't do it,' says a voice.

You twirl around to see a guy who's a bit older than you, carrying two ice glasses on an ice tray.

'I was smelling it,' you say, stepping away from the wall.

'Sure,' he smirks. 'Watch this.'

He presses the white napkin that hangs over his arm to the ice wall and signs for you to pull it.

You yank it off with a loud rip. Your tongue curls up in imagined pain.

'Thanks,' you mumble. 'I'm a ranger.'

He drops the ice tray and glasses. Red liquid flows out and freezes instantly into a large, flat puddle on the ice floor. 'I better clean this up.' He runs down the hallway.

Either he is a neat freak, or he didn't want to stick around when he found out you're a ranger. Why?

Turn to page 57

You find Rigmor sitting in the kitchen with a mug of steaming coffee. The heated kitchen is in a type of log teepee at the side of the ice hotel.

'There you are,' she says. 'This is my old friend, Inga, the chef here.'

A tall, very blonde woman shakes your hand in its fur glove. She wears simple rubber kitchen gloves and an insulated coverall. 'Come, have a drink.'

She holds out a square glass made of ice. You remember the napkin. 'Maybe later,' you say.

She laughs. 'It's safe. Any impurities and oxygen are removed from the water before it's frozen to make the glass, so your lips and tongue won't stick to it.'

'I really need a hot drink to warm up,' you say, quickly. You sit beside Rigmor at the kitchen table. An old man sits up the other end, cutting up mounds of cabbage. 'Hi,' you say.

He nods, but keeps chopping.

The door swings open and the clumsy waiter walks in.

'Svend,' says Inga. 'I told Rigmor you work part-time at the mining company adjacent to the national park. I've heard weird things about the owner. He claims to be a Viking and runs cultural tours in a Viking longship. I've tried to go on one, but it's always booked out.'

Turn to page 58

'I don't know anything,' mutters Svend. He slips off his fur gloves and coat, and puts on an apron. He, too, wears a pair of insulated coveralls.

'Maybe you can help us stop the blue whales beaching in the national park, Svend. Many die when they become marooned. Blue whales are an extremely endangered species. Any information helps,' says Rigmor.

Svend shrugs, picks up a knife, and joins the old man at the kitchen table. 'Move over, Julius,' he complains. 'No-one will get any meals if I don't help you chop the vegetables. You're so slow.'

You try. 'Svend, have you seen a blue whale? It's the largest creature to live on Earth, even bigger than any species of dinosaurs. Do you know its tongue weighs as much as an adult elephant and about one hundred people can fit inside its mouth?'

Svend stops chopping leeks. 'Why would anyone want to stand in a whale's mouth? I tell you, I know nothing. I only do a bit of work for the mining company.'

'You don't want to be working there, Svend lad,' says Julius in a creaky voice. 'Them, nasty creatures out there.'

'Whales?'

'No. Sea monsters,' says Julius. 'We call them the *kraken* around these parts.'

Turn to page 59

'Go back to your chopping, old man,' snaps Svend. 'That's foolish talk.'

'I wouldn't say that,' says Inga. 'The kraken may have some basis in truth. Some experts believe the legend was based on giant squids.'

'But what are the kraken?' you ask.

'Sea monsters of gargantuan size that lived off the coasts of Norway and Iceland,' says Rigmor. 'They were as big as a three-kilometre island, with many long tentacles. When a kraken submerged, it created a huge whirlpool that formed enormous ring waves, and any nearby ships sunk.'

'It's like I said,' says Julius. 'Unexplained waves and noises. The kraken ... The kraken has come back. Some say it signals the end of days when the kraken awakes.'

'I'm not paid enough to listen to this rubbish, Inga,' says Svend. He rips off his apron and storms through the door back into the ice hotel.

If you decide to follow him, turn to page 60
If you stay in the kitchen with Rigmor and the others,
turn to page 92

59

You need to follow him. Your ranger instinct warns you that he could be a clue to the mystery of the whale beachings. Also, he's so annoying you almost want him to be up to something. You don't trust Svend at all.

He thunders up the ice stairs and you slink after him. He pulls out a mobile phone and disappears into a room.

Quickly, you sneak up and press your ear against the reindeer hide that covers the ice door.

You can't hear a thing. The door is solid ice.

What if you melted a small hole in the ice? You snatch out the box of matches you always keep in your pocket for emergencies.

You strike a match that fizzes alight. You hold your breath because it sounds so loud in the quietness of the hallway. Svend could dash out any second and find you kneeling at the door. You need an excuse. With trembling fingers, you untie a shoelace. You can pretend to be tying up your boot.

Turn to page 62

Seconds go past, and the flame burns down the match. You drop it before it burns your fingers.

You light another match, lean down and hold the tiny, yellow flame to the bottom of the door. One minuscule droplet of water collects on the ice. This is going to take a long time.

After lighting more than twenty matches, you've had it. No sign of a hole, just a slightly moist section on the door. In frustration, you jab it with your finger.

The door opens slightly. You stare through the tiny crack. Svend isn't visible, but you hear him.

'Okay, *ja, ja,* yes. Room 143. I'll wait in this room until you arrive.'

Excellent. All you need to do is hide in the room opposite to see who does arrive.

You feel someone behind you.

You turn your head and see a pair of boots and legs about ten centimetres away.

If you make a run for it, turn to page 64
If you pretend to be doing up your boot, turn to page 63

'Whoops,' you say in a loud voice. 'Sorry, didn't see you standing there.'

Your heart beats so loudly, you're sure the tall man gazing down at you can hear it.

You grab the ends of your shoelace. 'Didn't want to trip over.'

He studies you as if you're a rare type of reindeer and he's the hunter. Your skin prickles.

You don't like this at all. Suddenly, you change your mind.

63

Turn to page 64

From page 62 and page 63

Surprise is your only defence in this situation. You jump up and race towards the staircase where you crash on the hard, icy floor.

You forgot about one untied shoelace.

Seconds later you're bundled up in reindeer hide from off a door, and lugged down the stairs. A scarf gags you so efficiently that you can't even squeak audibly.

You kick and struggle, but the man ignores you and carries you as if you're a dead reindeer. The blood rushes to your head as you dangle upside down.

The man stops and whispers, 'Svend, I'll go out the front door. You go to the kitchen and keep the others there.'

'What if they want to leave?' asks Svend.

'I'm sure you can think of something. A Viking is ingenious and quick-witted.'

A Viking?

Turn to page 65

You're outside. The man tosses you onto something hard.

You kick your legs and whack something.

Someone winces. 'If you do things like that, I'm not going to be very happy. And I warn you, you don't want to be near an unhappy Erik the Viking.'

A rope tightens around your legs until you can't budge them even a millimetre. You try to move your arms, but you can't pull them out because the reindeer hide is wrapped so tightly around you. It's suffocating, especially with the gag in your mouth.

An engine starts up, and whatever you're lying on vibrates. You must be in a car or truck.

A door slams and the vehicle shifts slowly forward.

'Hey, Erik!' yells Svend.

Turn to page 66

You hear footsteps and then a door slams. Svend must be inside the car with Erik.

'Hey,' says Rigmor's voice. 'What have you got in the back of your truck, driver?'

The truck halts. A door swings open with a soft creak.

'I asked what you have here, driver,' demands Rigmor. She sounds very near. 'I'm a ranger and responsible for all national parks, including this one.'

'My name is Erik,' says a bored-sounding voice. 'I'm the owner of the mining company that is working locally. You can be assured that I follow every law and restriction to the letter. Just now I need to take care of an urgent problem back at headquarters. I expect you know my young worker, Svend. I like to provide work in the local community.'

'Just lift up the tarpaulin, sir,' says Rigmor.

You're about to be rescued.

Turn to page 67

You hear a clicking sound as if the corner of a tarpaulin is being unattached. You must be in the tray of a truck.

'As you observe, it's a reindeer. Its head will look magnificent in my hunting lounge. Here's my permit to hunt in the national park.'

You hear a rustle of paper. 'All right, but remember the amount of game you kill is strictly monitored. If you are greedy ...'

'I know, I know,' says Erik. 'I will be fined, and you and your ranger colleagues are only protecting the natural environment and heritage of Norway.'

You wriggle as hard as you can, but you barely move. Surely Rigmor realises that it's not a real reindeer – just a skin wrapped around you!

67

You hear more clicks as if the tarpaulin is being fastened back down.

This isn't right. You need to be rescued.

You scream into the scarf until your eyes feel as if they are about to pop out. All you get out is a slight grunt and a minuscule groan.

'What's that?' asks Rigmor sharply.

'Svend,' says Erik, 'what did I tell you about your singing? Only do it in your own shower and have pity on all our ears.'

Turn to page 68

You strain against the scarf and grunt in your throat.

A door swings open. 'How was that?' asks Svend. 'I'm practising being a ventriloquist. Did you hear a noise in the back of the truck? I'm getting good, aren't I?'

'Excellent, don't you agree, ranger? But perhaps make it sound less like a constipated reindeer. I'm training Svend to copy the noises of animals, so he can be a sort of lure when we hunt.'

You wriggle, and manage to rock slightly. One, two, three rocks and you manage to flip over and get an arm free.

'Well, don't encourage him to bark like a wolf,' says Rigmor.

Your arm has pins and needles from lying on it for so long. You flex your fingers and hold out your hand ready to bang on the side of the truck.

Rigmor continues, 'Wolf packs drive me crazy with their constant barking. Woof, woof, woof, all day and night.'

If you bang on the side of the truck to get Rigmor's attention, turn to page 84
If you decide to lie quietly, turn to page 70

From page 33

Guilt floods you. If you had listened to Rigmor in the first place there would be no avalanche, and she wouldn't be in an ice cave, trying not to whimper in pain.

Once she falls asleep you'll search for help. If you walk along a stream, you should eventually come to a town, or cross over a road. This area isn't that isolated.

You lie beside Rigmor and wait for her to drift off to sleep. She wants to talk, but you pretend to be asleep.

Eventually, she drops off, but every so often she cries out in pain.

'Goodnight, and goodbye, Rigmor,' you murmur.

Outside is black. You turn on your torch; although it's a puny light, you don't feel as alone.

Your stomach grumbles loudly. You would eat anything right now, even cooked carrots and you hate them. You feel hot, which is weird because the temperature must be freezing.

You search for a stream, but you only see snow.

You trudge on. Your ears fill with a swishing noise like the wings of a million flying moths. You shake your head. Maybe if you sit down for a second your mind will clear. Just for a minute. You'll get up very soon ...

69

THE END

From page 68

You pull your arm back.

What a weird thing for Rigmor to say. The grey wolves found in Norway only bark when nervous or when alerting other wolves to danger; they don't bark loudly or repeatedly like dogs do. Wolves howl much more often than they bark. Rigmor must know that.

Relief oozes through you. She knows you're in the back of the truck, and this is her way of telling you.

You listen carefully as she continues, 'Take care on your trip back to headquarters. It's getting dark. I'll see you all very soon.'

You want to shout, 'Message received, loud and clear', but instead you lie quietly. Rigmor's going to rescue you soon, but in the meantime you'll see what you can find out about Erik and his mining operations.

Turn to page 71

From page 70

The truck starts up, and speeds along a straight road. You're warm in your fake fur coat and soon doze off.

You wake up when a torch flashes in your face.

'Young ranger, you seem very relaxed to be in my power,' says Erik. 'I have to ask myself, are you stupid or do you know something I don't?'

'Jetlag. I arrived today. Don't hurt me.' You look scared. It's not difficult, because you are.

'Men, throw our visitor in the dinghy.'

Seconds later, you sprawl on the bottom of a boat.

'Untie the ranger,' says Erik. 'I want to observe our young friend's reaction.'

After the ropes and reindeer hide are removed, you sit up nervously beside Svend on a wooden bench. Erik sits next to the tiller, and four other men row the boat away from the jetty.

The full moon lights up the sea like a film set. You stare at the dark, still water. There's not even a ripple.

Suddenly, you hear a muffled rumble, and huge, circular waves break the water. The dinghy rocks up and down. You grip your seat so you don't fall out.

The water churns. Something's about to surface. Is it the kraken or sea monster that Julius warned you about back at the ice hotel?

Turn to page 72

The surface of the sea bubbles and something black emerges.

Oh boy. You know what to do with most animals, but sea monsters are completely different. You hold your breath and wait.

The long, streamlined body of a submarine surfaces.

You breathe out slowly. That explains all the whales beaching. The sonar waves from the submarine would confuse the whales, because they rely on their own sonar system for navigation.

'What a most satisfactory reaction!' says Erik. 'Has old Julius been telling his tales of sea monsters? I encourage it, since it keeps people away. My sub lays down explosives as you witnessed, and then I discover what minerals are available. I expect to strike oil soon. That old kraken myth has proven most handy to explain away noises and unusual wave patterns.'

'I wasn't scared even a tiny bit,' you lie.

'You were as white as freshly fallen snow,' says Svend.

'I get seasick. That's probably why I looked pale.'

Svend smirks.

A mobile phone rings loudly. You recognise the tune. It's 'Yellow Submarine'.

'Yes. Talk to me,' barks Erik.

Turn to page 74

The speaker murmurs too softly for you to be able to distinguish any words.

Erik frowns and glances at you uneasily.

'Deal with it.' Erik snaps his phone shut. 'You lot, row faster if you don't want me to tip you in the water. Thor's thunder, you're pathetic.'

The four men lean over their oars, and the dinghy flies up and down the waves until it pulls up alongside the submarine. The sub resembles a strange bird of prey, waiting to unfurl its wings and pounce.

'Jump on board,' orders Erik.

You hesitate. Once you're on board the submarine, it will be like being trapped inside a tin can without a can opener. Also, it's going to be a whole lot more difficult for Rigmor and the other rangers to rescue you.

You stare down at the inky, cold, black sea. Even though the shore is close, hypothermia – the rapid and abnormal chilling of the body – could kill you in less than ten minutes in these icy waters.

One of the submariners holds out a hand to you.

You take a deep breath.

Erik jumps lightly onto the submarine. 'Your turn, ranger.'

If you board the submarine, turn to page 76
If you jump into the icy waters, turn to page 140

You really don't like the way the man glances from the gleaming blade of his sword, then directly at you.

You need to get out of here. You spin around and head towards a gap in the trees. You force yourself to trudge onwards, even though with each step your boots sink deeper and deeper into the snow.

You stumble into a clearing. Everything is white. Suddenly, the sun breaks through the clouds, turning the snow into blinding diamonds that dazzle you.

'I'm Erik,' says a voice that sounds very close, too close. 'I didn't introduce myself before when we met.'

You squint over your shoulder and see what looks like a traditional Viking, but wearing sunglasses.

'I'm the last person you'll ever meet,' says Erik. 'I would say, next time look out for an ambush. But there will be no more next times for you, my little ranger friend.'

You see a flash of silver.

THE END

You leap onto the deck of the submarine.

'Come on,' shouts Erik, who stands on top of the conning tower.

You follow, and clamber down the narrow, metal ladder into a small chamber with huge windows and watertight steel doors at each end. The four men who rowed the boat slip through one door. You glimpse engines and pipes. That must be the inner hull, which is surrounded by large ballast tanks.

Valves on the top of the ballast tanks open when the submarine submerges, allowing air in the tanks to escape, and holes at the bottom of the tanks let seawater flood in. Water is heavier than air, so the submarine 'sinks'.

'Sit.' Erik flips down a metal chair attached to a wall.

You sit, and he ties you up quickly and efficiently.

He says, 'Svend, tonight's the night you can be in charge of the periscope. If you see any boats, let me know fast. I'm off to supervise the laying of the charges. I've got a feeling that I'm going to unearth some very special mineral deposits tonight.'

Svend smiles. 'I won't let you down, Erik.'

Erik slaps him on the back and disappears into the inner hull.

Svend marches over to the periscope in the middle of the room.

Turn to page 77

The submarine submerges, and Svend stares into the periscope.

'You should swivel the periscope around, Svend. Then you can look in every direction. The word "periscope" comes from the Greek words *peri* meaning "around" and *scopus* meaning "to look".'

'Quiet, I'm concentrating.' But Svend starts swivelling the periscope around.

Then it strikes you. Why did you say that? Rigmor and your other rescuers will find it harder to approach now.

Blip ... blip ... blip.

You freeze. You know what that sound means. Erik's turned on the active sonar. Sonar has been linked to many whale strandings.

'Do you like nature, Svend?'

'What?' Svend mumbles.

'Trees, snow, fish and whales?'

'Whales are fish, smarty.' Svend remains glued to the periscope.

'They're not fish. They're mammals. When a whale dies, all the other whales mourn. They look after their young for years. The sonar sound waves from this sub drown out the noises that whales need for survival ...'

'Visitors,' says Svend, pulling down the periscope.

Turn to page 78

'Don't tell him,' you say desperately.

'He'll kill me if I don't.'

The sub moves slightly as something swims past. The light from the room shines on a blue whale.

You gasp. Talk about fantastic timing. 'Take a look, Svend.'

Svend looks up from the periscope and then creeps to the window. If there was no glass in the window, he could touch the whale.

The whale is a true blue colour underwater, but on the surface it often looks more blue-grey. The underbelly has a yellowish tinge from the millions of micro-organisms that live on its skin. It's thirty metres long and must weigh more that 181 tonnes. A huge moan fills the cabin.

'Blue whales can hear each other up to 1600 kilometres away,' you say, 'they live for eighty to ninety years. Over 360,000 blue whales were slaughtered between 1900 and the 1960s. They're extremely endangered now. They rely on sonar to survive, but the sonar from this sub and the illegal explosion of mines confuses marine animals. It's up to us to save them.'

The door swings open. 'Not at your post?' asks Erik.

'I just left it.' Svend scurries back.

'Anything to report,' asks Erik, 'apart from the oversized blubber outside?'

You hold your breath.

Turn to page 80

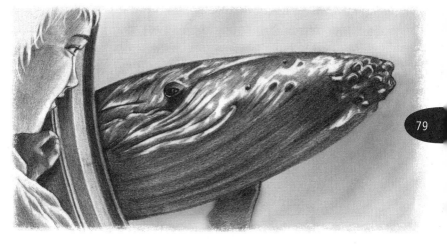

'Nothing,' says Svend.

'Good. When we surface, young ranger, I'll put you in the ballast tanks. Then, when the valves open, you'll swish into the deep sea with all the water. Back soon.'

You want to throw up.

'What do we do now?' asks Svend, after Erik leaves the chamber.

'Can we lock that door somehow?' You stare at the steel door, but unfortunately there's no lock.

You remember the game of hide-and-seek that you played when you were little. Seekers would look around on the ground, but often miss people who had climbed up something high, even when they were in clear view.

'Svend, here's an idea. It may not be a good idea, but it will have to do. Untie me and then I'll climb up to the top of the periscope. With a bit of luck, Erik won't notice me because he'll be too busy looking at you, lying unconscious under the periscope.'

Svend looks doubtful. 'For a start, can you even climb up there?' He looks at the periscope.

'Part of ranger training is learning to climb. Let's face it, Svend, this plan's the only chance we've got.'

Turn to page 81

Two minutes later, you shimmy up to the top of the periscope and Svend lies below it. Minutes pass.

Svend stands up. 'This won't work. We need to get Erik here. You forgot that, mastermind.'

'Pass me up the chair,' you say. 'When I fling the metal chair down from this height, it will be loud enough to awaken the kraken.'

Seconds later, you cling onto the periscope pole with one hand, and hold the chair in the other hand.

'Action stations,' you whisper.

Svend crumples to the floor and you toss down the metal chair.

Crash!

The door bursts open. 'Thor's thunder, Svend.' Erik stops and dashes over to Svend. He's directly under the periscope.

You hurtle downwards and pull both the periscope and yourself onto Erik's head. Svend rolls out of the way, and pulls out the rope he stuffed up his jumper.

Within one minute, Erik's tied up to the periscope.

You smile at Svend and shake hands.

'Men!' screams Erik.

Whoops. You forgot all about them.

Turn to page 82

The four men thunder into the room. They stop when they see Erik tied up to the periscope.

You and Svend slink away towards the other door. It's your only hope.

'Halt,' orders the tallest and biggest man.

You both stop.

'You two might want to see this.' He strides over to Erik.

'Untie me at once, then we'll place them in the ballast tanks,' screams Erik. 'They both deserve to die.'

You grip Svend's hand.

'I don't think so, Erik,' says the tall man. 'Watch this.'

He pushes the periscope up until Erik rises high into the air. 'You think you're so high and mighty and above us all, Erik. What's it like looking down from up there?'

Everyone laughs, except for one notable exception.

Erik snarls. 'You'll all be sorry one day.'

'Thor's thunder,' you say. 'I thought being a good loser was the Viking way.'

THE END

You ball your hand into a fist, and bang the side of the truck as hard as you can.

'Okay, guys,' says Rigmor. 'I'll be seeing you.'

What's wrong with her? She must have heard.

The truck starts up and you travel along a windy, bumpy road. Luckily, the fake fur coat and reindeer hide absorb most of the bumps.

Finally, the truck stops and the doors swing open.

'Come on, Svend, time to secure this ranger.'

They pass a rope under your stomach a few times, then draw it tight. You can't move. You feel like a huge, wrapped-up parcel of fake fur.

'You did us a favour,' says Erik. 'Rigmor obviously suspects you're in here because she, more than anyone, knows that wolves don't bark incessantly like dogs, but only give a soft bark when frightened or warning of danger. She was clumsily hinting to you that she knew you were there.'

Shame floods you. Of course. Erik is quite right.

He continues, 'Then not to hear when you banged on the side of the truck. Thor's thunder, she takes me for a fool. She'll be sorry. Of course, she'll follow us and then she'll learn no-one triumphs over Erik the Viking.'

Turn to page 85

Erik laughs, sounding as if he's a maniac in a horror film, but instead of laughing like you normally do when you watch these films, your blood runs cold. And what is this Viking stuff? He can't really believe he's a Viking.

The truck starts up and veers off to the right. You slam into the side of the truck's tray, but it doesn't hurt because the fur coat and reindeer hide protect you. You try to release your arms, but the ropes around you are too tight.

The truck slows to a stop. You hear doors slam shut. A few seconds later, you're lifted out. Frantically, you try to kick and struggle, but you're trapped by your fur wrappings.

Erik and Svend toss you onto a snowy track. You groan deep in your throat, even though it didn't really hurt because of the insulating fur.

'Are you okay?' asks Svend.

'Svend, Svend, Svend,' says Erik. 'A Viking must think of his purpose and not worry about insignificant people along the way.'

You feel the thump of a kick. It doesn't hurt a bit, but you groan and wriggle as if you're in agony.

'That's how it's done,' announces Erik. 'Soon Rigmor will walk into our trap.'

85

Turn to page 86

Svend drags you along the track, and you groan at every bump. You're not sure but you think you hear a muttered, 'Sorry'.

Finally, you stop. Erik unties your gag and pulls down your fur coverings so you can see clearly.

You look down a sheer cliff into a glacier. You're not sure what's going to happen next, but you're sure you won't like it.

'Rigmor won't fall for your trick,' you say.

You hear the distant sound of a car pulling up.

'Won't she, indeed?' asks Erik, with a wolfish smile.

'Rig ...!' you scream, before Svend claps his hand tightly over your mouth.

Erik disappears into the woods with a length of rope.

Minutes later, he emerges with a struggling Rigmor, who is wrapped up in some sort of reindeer snare. He deposits her next to you on the edge of the precipice.

'Sorry,' she says. 'I can't believe I trod in that snare and ended up hanging upside down from a tree.'

Together, you stare into the glacier, its whiteness glowing in the fading light.

Turn to page 87

'This is what happens to my enemies. You bring in laws so I can't mine where I want, and fuss over blue whales beaching. It's not my fault the stupid pieces of blubber get confused by soundwaves caused by my exploratory blasting on the seafloor.' He stops and pulls something out of his backpack.

It's a metal helmet with two horns sticking out. He puts it on. 'Nor is it my fault that you rangers poked your noses into my business. I am Erik the Viking. I live by my own rules.'

'You need to check your Viking history,' says Rigmor, sounding calm, but you can see a vein throb at her temple. 'The real Vikings wore helmets with a metal tongue stretching down over their noses for protection. The horns were something dreamt up in the nineteenth century.'

Erik's face blooms red. 'I wear this outfit as part of my grand plan. I run cultural tours in my Viking longship, and no-one suspects I'm really checking out the waters of the national parks. Svend, toss them into the glacier,' he says, turning away.

'Wait,' says Rigmor. 'We can sort this out.'

'Goodbye. You have both now officially expired.'

'Svend,' you plead. 'Don't do it.'

If you can't convince Svend not to throw you both into the glacier, turn to page 88
If you can convince Svend not to throw you both into the glacier, turn to page 151

87

From page 87

'Wait,' you say.

Svend hesitates, but steps towards you with outstretched arms.

Erik nods approvingly. 'Svend, watch me.'

You feel a push, then you tumble through the air, landing with a thud on the glacier. You wince as you hear Rigmor crash beside you.

Amazingly, you feel unhurt, but something warns you to lie there quietly. You'll be like the Arctic fox, which pretends to be dead to fool its predators.

'Climb down and check on them,' says Erik from the top of the cliff.

You hear a jangle of metal and Svend abseils down the cliff. He slides across the glacier surface to Rigmor. 'She's alive,' he yells.

Relief floods through you.

Turn to page 89

'But she broke a leg, judging by its angle, and one of her hands is twisted around the wrong way,' Svend yells.

'She won't last the night on the glacier with those injuries,' says Erik. 'And the little ranger?'

You lie still thinking, 'Arctic fox, Arctic fox', but you know there's no way you'll fool Svend when he's so close to you. He squats beside you.

You try to keep still, but your lips tremble with the effort.

'This ranger's dead,' shouts Svend.

You open one eye slightly. Svend licks his lips nervously, but yells, 'The fall was fatal.'

'Good, Svend. Get back up here. I didn't want to waste a bullet on either ranger,' calls out Erik.

Svend shimmies back up the cliff.

You wait until you can't hear them anymore, and then call out softly, 'Rigmor.'

89

Turn to page 90

'What?' she asks in a husky voice. 'Am I hearing voices?'

You rock yourself from side to side and eventually flip over again and again until you roll up to Rigmor.

She stares at you with watery eyes. 'You're not dead?'

'Not at all. Untie me and I'll get out of this giant cocoon.'

Quickly, Rigmor fishes out her ranger knife and uses her one good hand to hack at your bindings. The ropes fall off and you're free.

You gaze up at the steep cliffs surrounding the glacier, which runs along the bottom of a valley. No way can you climb up there without ropes or crampons.

'Don't worry,' says Rigmor. 'With my skills, we'll survive the night on the glacier. Help me over there.' She points to where a stream runs down the cliff. 'The stream formed a huge ice cave where it runs under the glacier. With your furs and reindeer hide, we'll be warmish and sheltered for the night.'

The glacier creaks and groans as you grab hold of Rigmor. Luckily, you're in a slow-moving section, judging by the smooth terrain, so there's less chance of parts of the glacier breaking off. You slip and slide as you help Rigmor to the glacier cave.

When you reach it, Rigmor is panting and very white. Every part of your body feels bruised because the glacier was as hard as steel when you fell on it.

Turn to page 91

Inside, the cave is amazing. Your torch picks up the intense, bright blue of its walls and the semi-circle of a roof. It's about ten metres long, and protects you from the icy wind and any possible snow falls.

You lay the reindeer hide on the icy surface and spread the fake fur coat over you both. You insist Rigmor wears the fur hat to help prevent loss of body heat.

'What do we do now?' you ask.

'Soon I will be reported missing. Ranger headquarters can hack into the GPS in the jeep and discover its whereabouts. Then we will prosecute Erik for his crimes and the blue whales will be saved.'

You snuggle down under the fur coat. You remember how Svend pretended that you were dead. 'And Svend. I think he'll return for us. He's no Evil Erik.'

'Let us hope so,' says Rigmor. 'We need every person we can get to help us fight for the natural environment. But if he doesn't help, he too will be charged.'

'Hello,' echoes around the glacier. It's Svend. 'I couldn't leave you here.'

Rigmor smiles. 'You were right. He truly is no Evil Erik, after all.'

THE END

From page 59

'What's up with him?' you say. 'Svend has a problem.'

'I know,' says Julius. 'I'm his grandfather. This Erik arrived and promised us riches if we let him mine our lands and the waters of our sea. I refused and my house burnt down. Luckily, Inga offered me lodging here.'

Inga gasps. 'I thought sparks from the stove were responsible. You never told me you suspected Erik.'

'I'm holding my tongue until I have something. Erik runs cultural Viking longship tours as a sideline. He claims to be the last remaining Viking. I didn't want Svend working there, but he won't listen. Says he's learning how to be a Viking.' Julius shakes his head.

'What else do you know about Erik?' asks Rigmor.

'He likes to hunt,' says Julius, 'and run around in a tin helmet with two horns sticking out. He doesn't realise the helmet and horns thing was an invention in the nineteenth century to attract people to the opera.'

You, Rigmor, Inga and Julius all laugh.

'Does he sing?' snorts Rigmor.

Julius smiles, then looks sad. 'Lately people disappear, houses burn down, ancient rivers silt up from his mining operations and there are no salmon. For hundreds of years, my family's living has been salmon.'

'We'll help you.' You yawn. 'But maybe in the morning.'

Turn to page 93

You lie snug in your ice bed. It's just daylight. You're busting to go to the toilet, but that will mean leaving the warmth of the reindeer skins and your insulated sleeping bag.

You distract yourself by remembering all the yummy food you ate last night. Pickled herrings that stank like a rubbish bin left out for a week but were amazingly delicious – as long as you held your nose. *Multekrem* for dessert, which is cloudberries, a very juicy, yellowish-green berry, with cream. Then a yummy chocolate milk drink called *freia melkesjolodade*.

Why did you think about drink? You can't wait any longer. You leap from the bed, and run down the hallway to the bathroom block on the ground floor, flicking on lights as you go. Luckily, you're wearing the provided fake fur-lined sleeping boots so you don't need to waste time putting on shoes ...

As you wash your hands, a shadow appears on the bathroom blind. It's a figure with two horns sticking out of its head. It could be Erik, the Viking, or even Svend, Viking-in-training. Or maybe there are other supposed Vikings roaming around the national park.

You debate whether to lift up the blind or not.

Do you want him or her to see you? What's anyone doing here so early?

If you open the blind, turn to page 94
If you leave the blind down, turn to page 100

93

From page 93

You yank the blind and it spins upwards.

Outside, you see snow and nothing else. Hold on. A wolf – no, it's a tamaskan husky picking its way through the snow. Tamaskans were bred to resemble wolves and have a bushy, wolf-like tail.

Inga told you about the hotel's teams of huskies last night, but she didn't mention that she had tamaskans, which are a relatively rare breed. They're famous for being excellent search-and-rescue dogs, with good endurance, agility, and a keen sense of smell.

The dog saunters towards the window. Red covers its back leg. It's injured.

You fly out of the hotel, just as the dog trots towards the woods.

'Wait!' you call. You wish you knew the Norwegian word for 'stop', but you don't.

The dog ignores you. How did it get injured? Would Erik or Svend injure a dog?

Inga suggested last night that you take a team of huskies to the national park. Is this Erik's brutal way of trying to make you stay away?

You charge after the dog and run into the woods.

Turn to page 96

From page 94

Inside the woods, snow blankets the whole world in silence. You follow the tracks of the dog. It mustn't be bleeding too profusely, as there's no blood trail.

You wind in and out between the birch trees, which are covered in tiny, fluorescent green buds. You see a perfectly round frozen pond.

You hold your breath as you watch a white Arctic fox saunter along the snow and onto the pond. The thickly furred pads of its feet provide traction on the ice.

The Arctic fox jumps up and down, until the ice breaks under its front paws. Quickly, it grabs a wriggling lemming, a type of rodent. You've heard this is how an Arctic fox sometimes hunts, but it's amazing to actually observe this behaviour.

You shake yourself. You need to help the dog. You speed onwards after its tracks.

Finally, you see the dog. It sits beside the skis of a man dressed in a deer-trimmed, wool cape. On top of his head, the man wears a helmet with two horns.

96

Turn to page 97

From page 96

'Your animal, it's injured.' You point to the bloody leg.

The man pulls a cloth from a pocket of his pants and wipes off the blood. 'Actually, it would be more appropriate if I wiped it off with a pie or chips.'

You stare at him. No more blood appears.

The man laughs. 'Allow me to introduce myself. I'm Erik, the last of the true Vikings. You didn't think I would deliberately injure my own dog, Ludvik? It's tomato sauce, and you, my little ranger, just fell for one of the oldest tricks in the book. I watched you rush to the bathroom, a very easy task as you turned on every light to mark your route. Then I paraded myself outside the blind and sure enough you opened the blind in time to see Ludvik.'

Your cheeks burn, but you lift up your chin and stare directly at Erik. 'What do you want with me?'

'It's up to you. If you're prepared to act as a double agent, and report back on what Rigmor finds out, you'll be very useful to me.'

'And if I don't agree?'

Erik shakes his head sorrowfully. 'Don't even think of going there.'

If you decide to stall, turn to page 98
If you agree to be a double agent, turn to page 131

From page 97

You cover your face with your hands. Slowly, an idea forms in your brain. It might not be the most reliable idea you've ever had, but you go with it. 'This is a lot to take in,' you say.

'There will be rewards.' Erik smiles, wolfishly.

'It's not safe to talk here,' you whisper. 'Anyone could be behind the trees listening to us.'

Erik laughs. 'Ludvik would warn us.'

'If I'm going to commit to being a double agent, I'll do a good job, and I think we should start as we mean to go on. We need to talk somewhere out in the open, so we know nobody is eavesdropping.'

Erik shrugs.

'What about back here? I passed a frozen pond. We'll see anyone who approaches,' you say.

Erik and Ludvik follow you back to the pond where you watched the Arctic fox earlier.

A light cover of snow lies on the surface. Desperately, you try to guess where the Arctic fox jumped on the ice.

'Let's stand here,' you announce.

Turn to page 99

From page 98

Erik stares at you, but moves exactly where you want him. 'You're a funny fish, little ranger. But if this helps you be a good double agent, I'll go along with it.'

Suddenly, you push Erik backwards and he lands with a thump. The ice cracks and he falls into the water below.

'You're a funnier fish, Erik! Earlier I saw an Arctic fox jump up and down on the snow just near where you are. I hoped that this would weaken the ice in the immediate area, and it did.'

'Help me out!' shouts Erik.

'So, you don't want me as an employee?' you ask.

'I would rather freeze to death,' he spits out.

'Erik,' you say. 'That wouldn't actually be too hard to arrange now that you're paddling in a frozen pond. But, once you're in jail, it will be a bit harder for you to ruin the streams with your mining operations.'

Erik snarls as if he's an extremely bad-tempered wolverine.

You smile. 'You're lucky I am a ranger and protect all animals – even the nasty ones like you.'

THE END

From page 93

As tempting as it is, you don't pull up the blind. You don't want Erik to realise that you know he's out there. Instead, you sneak out of the bathroom and into the kitchen.

Rigmor, Inga and Julius sit around the kitchen table, eating muesli.

'I saw Erik,' you say.

Rigmor stands up. 'Where?'

'Through the blind, outside the bathroom window. I'm guessing it was Erik. It was someone wearing a horned helmet.'

Inga and Julius leap up.

'No,' says Rigmor. 'You two stay here. We'll go and check it out.'

Outside, it's snowing lightly. You trudge around to the bathroom window. A wooden sword lies in the snow. It's broken in half.

Rigmor pales. 'A broken sword is an old Viking warning for you not to go there or else there'll be war.'

'Go where?' you ask.

'Guessing, I would say the national park,' says Rigmor. 'We can either do my usual patrol to count reindeer and be watchful, or make a concerted effort to find this Erik. It's your choice.'

If you decide to do the usual patrol, but be watchful, turn to page 154
If you decide to hunt Erik, turn to page 101

Julius wraps an orange wool scarf around you. 'This will bring you good luck. It has been in my family many years and it is passed down once there is a worthy family member to wear it. In the meantime, I wish you to borrow it.'

Briefly, you clasp his hand.

One of your dogs barks and you pick up the leads. Rigmor decided to use sleds to reach the national park, so Erik has no warning of your arrival along the track.

'Ready to go?' asks Rigmor.

You nod. 'Come on!' you shout. 'Let's go.'

Your team of eight huskies shoots after Rigmor. It's fantastic zooming along the snow. The dogs pull you up and over a huge hill as if it's no bigger than a speed hump.

Rigmor points to a clump of firs about twenty metres away. You hush the barking dogs and watch a two-metre tall brown bear stagger out. It looks cute – just like the one that used to sit on your bed, except this bear is capable of taking on a wolf pack and winning.

As this region warms, the potential habitat of the brown bear increases and the bears will roam further north into areas where the polar bear used to be the only bear. Any potential habitat further south has decreased, due to human activities. That's why national parks are so important. Erik can't destroy them.

Turn to page 102

Rigmor pulls up and you glide to a stop beside her.

You gaze at the fjord below. A glittering blue, narrow inlet flows between high cliffs. Partially frozen waterfalls form pale-blue ice columns that water cascades down inside and churns up the sea.

'It's beautiful,' you say. A family group of four harp seals waddle across a pebble beach. Black harp shapes mark their silvery-grey backs.

'Erik wanted to drill for oil in the park fjords. He doesn't care that oil spills hurt and even kill seals when their fur becomes coated in oil and they can't regulate their body temperature. Oil spills kill birds and other marine life too; many seals die from starvation because they lose their food supply.' Rigmor pulls out binoculars from her backpack. 'Check out their faces.'

The seals look sad. You know the cold wind irritates their eyes that are adapted for water, but still ...

'I need to protect them when I see their faces. I know they're not really crying, but they call me to help them,' says Rigmor.

A hard lump collects in your throat. You gulp.

A strange rumble breaks the silence. Huge bubbles burst into circular waves.

You don't believe in monsters, but you fear them. Is this the kraken?

Turn to page 104

'Quick,' says Rigmor.

You call out to your dogs, 'Let's go.' The dogs bark happily and you and Rigmor speed through the snow.

She steers a path through the woods, and you catch glimpses of blue sparkling water through the fir trees.

'Hush,' Rigmor instructs her dogs.

You quieten your dogs too, and stop beside her on the edge of the woods.

About twenty metres away, you see Svend fiddle with some sort of radio or phone in his hand. He stands in the middle of a track, standing guard.

You and Rigmor slide out of your sleds.

'We'll leave the huskies here,' she murmurs.

You dive into your pockets for dog treats, and the huskies lick them out of your hands. The huskies are big and wolf-like in appearance, but they're very gentle.

Rigmor signs for them to rest beside the sleds and they all hunker down immediately.

'What now?' you whisper.

'I'm not sure,' says Rigmor. 'I can't let my feelings for Svend's grandfather, Julius, influence me. You decide.'

If you approach Svend, turn to page 105
If you sneak past Svend to the beach, turn to page 112

'Let's give Svend a chance,' you say.

Rigmor nods and together you leave the forest.

Svend jumps when he sees you. His eyes are red-rimmed and he looks even sadder than the harp seals.

'Just listen,' you say. 'Svend, you're mixed up in something and ...'

'I was trying to contact you,' he bursts out. 'I didn't know. So many are dying. Please. Quick!'

You and Rigmor charge down the trail after him. You slip over in the snow once, but Svend yanks you up before you have time to get wet.

The trail opens onto an icy sandy beach. Nine humpback whales lie stranded on the shore. You stare at their rorquals, or throat grooves, and the long coarse sensor hair about fifteen metres long that grows out of the centre of each tubercle, or knob on their head.

It's too much. How can you save all the whales?

'Come on. The tide turns, all is not lost,' shouts Rigmor. 'We need to keep the whales wet. Any towels or buckets, Svend?'

'Erik keeps lots of supplies here.' Svend races up to a shed with a shiny, new padlock and a small window in one side. 'I don't have a key, and he would kill me if I went in there.'

Turn to page 106

From page 105

You pick up a piece of driftwood, then rip off your coat and hold it against the window. Whack! 'He'll kill me, not you, Svend. Help me up to the window. It's small, but I'll fit through it somehow.'

Inside, you find shovels, towels, blankets and buckets. You throw them back out the window.

'The main thing is to keep the whales wet until high tide.' Rigmor pulls out her phone. 'I'll call for reinforcements.'

Svend dashes down to the sea and scoops up a bucket of water. He swings it back, ready to empty it onto the nearest whale.

'Watch out for the blowholes, Svend. Don't put water there, because whales breathe through their blowholes and we don't want any whales with water on their lungs.'

Svend reddens, and turns to wet the towels in the sea.

Rigmor says, 'Svend. You've done a very brave thing. I'll thank you properly once we've sorted out this situation.'

Svend grins and races up and down with buckets as if he's competing in an Olympic event.

Turn to page 108

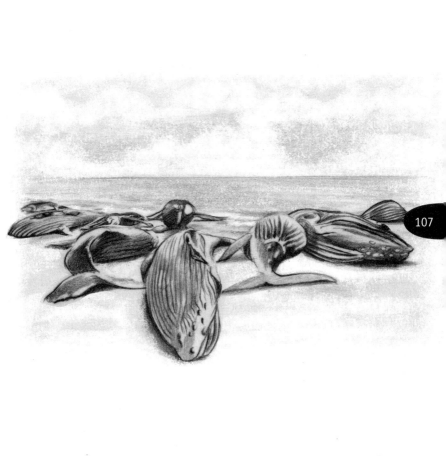

From page 106

Five jeeps pull up, and eleven rangers tumble out. They
run down the beach with buckets and swiftly begin
helping you keep the whales moist. Two start digging
channels down to the sea to make it easier for the
whales to swim out to sea when the tide comes in.

You check the sea. The waves are coming in.

Suddenly, the ground shakes and you hear a rumble.

'What's that?' shouts a ranger.

Svend flinches and looks down at his boots. He's
beside you, helping moisten the towels on the smallest
whale. 'Svend?'

'Erik,' he whispers. 'He's got a submarine for
exploratory mining.'

'What?' You explode.

Rigmor shouts, 'Leave it until later.'

Finally, you feel the sea splash around your ankles
and then your knees.

You all gently guide the whales back into the sea.
One, two, three, four, they all glide out, except the
smallest one.

'It must be injured,' you whisper.

Rigmor stands beside you. 'I'm sorry, but it's dying.'

Turn to page 109

Tears burn your eyes, but you talk to the whale, trying to comfort it. Svend helps you gently pour water over the whale's skin to keep it cool.

Eventually, it's still.

'You knew this was going on!' you scream at Svend. 'Why didn't you try to stop it?'

'Hush,' says Rigmor. 'Experts claim that often the internal organs of beached whales are harmed somehow by sonar waves or explosions. This poor whale faced both. It was probably always going to die, no matter what we did.'

You nod and move back up the beach. A jeep pulls up, and Inga and Julius climb out. 'Dry blankets, clothes and food,' shouts Inga.

You try to ignore your freezing wet clothes and stare out to sea. The water is still sparkling and blue.

Suddenly you see what looks like a black snake pop up. A periscope.

'Rigmor, we're being watched.'

'Then smile, like me.' Rigmor flashes a dazzling smile. 'The coastguard will arrive soon to arrest them. Erik won't be mining for a very long time. I wonder if they'll let him wear his special, supposed–Viking helmet in jail?'

'Where's Svend?' you ask.

Then you see him. He's standing by himself in the shallows. He must be freezing.

Turn to page 110

From page 109

You splash through the water. 'Svend?'

He studies the sand as if he's never seen it before.

'I'm sorry. You helped save ten whales. That's an unbelievable effort.'

'Erik promised me I would be a Viking like him.' Svend speaks so softly that you can hardly hear him. 'At first he taught me to shoot reindeer with a bow and arrow, just like my ancestors did. But then he made me go on the submarine with him while he searched for oil deposits. He said I was guilty too now, and nobody would believe that I didn't want to be involved in the mining.'

'I believe you and so will everyone else here,' you say. 'Let's join the others.'

You and Svend walk back up to a blazing fire.

Julius strides up to you and touches his orange scarf. 'May I?'

You hand it to him.

'Svend,' he says, 'I thought I had no-one worthy in my family to pass on this scarf to, but I was wrong.'

Julius ties the scarf tightly around Svend's neck and hugs him quickly.

'When you're both dry and warm, I'll tell you tales of the Viking times,' says Julius. 'I'm presuming you rangers are happy to celebrate for the rest of the day?'

Everyone cheers and the party begins.

THE END

All you need to do is keep calm.

You push the battery into the motor and grab the two leads. Your fingers shake as you connect first the black lead, then the red lead.

Erik and Lars are only two metres away.

You thrust down the lever and wait for the snowmobile to roar into life.

Nothing.

'Missing something?' asks Erik, holding out a petrol can.

You leap out of the snowmobile, but Lars grips your arm as tightly as a python.

'Why didn't you listen to my warning and return to your homeland, little ranger,' Erik says, pulling a long face. He shrugs. 'You leave me with no choice now, because you know my secrets.'

111

THE END

From page 104

You stare at Svend, who looks miserable. 'I'm not sure we can trust him. Let's sneak past.'

Rigmor nods and you both creep through the woods. The trail ends at a small, sandy beach. There is no sign of any cars. You notice a shed with its door propped open.

Marks in the icy sand show a boat was dragged over it. You stare out to sea.

The low, black silhouette of a submarine lurks in the water, and beside it is the weirdest boat you've ever seen. A post curls up from the ship's bow. 'Rigmor?'

She lifts up her binoculars and gasps. 'It's a Viking longship with a dragon's head carved into the fore post.'

'Erik,' you and Rigmor say together.

'It makes sense now,' says Rigmor. 'Erik could travel where he liked in his longship, pretending to conduct cultural tours. The longship would be the supply ship for the submarine. The sonar waves of the submarine interfere with the sonar of the whales. Because whales use sonar for navigation, feeding, everything, then the whales must get confused and beach themselves.'

You peer inside the shed. Neatly stacked explosives line the walls. 'Rigmor,' you call. 'You might want to go in the shed.'

'You might both want to go in the shed,' shouts a voice. Svend wears a Viking helmet with two horns, but points a very un-Viking looking gun at you.

Turn to page 113

'You could decide to help us, Svend,' says Rigmor.

'Erik promised me I'll be a true Viking too.'

Rigmor snorts. 'He is no true Viking. The Vikings only took what they needed and never any more. This national park's for everyone, yet Erik thinks he can lay explosives on the seafloor to search for oil. That's what he's searching for, isn't he?'

Svend gives a slight nod.

You glance out to sea. 'Rigmor, the boat's coming back.'

Quickly, you and Rigmor hide in the shed. You lift up a loose piece of timber near the entrance and peer out. Svend walks down the beach, and the boat being narrow and not very deep, sails right up to the shore.

Erik leaps out. 'I thought you were on guard. You don't seem as keen to be a Viking nowadays, young Svend. Your grandfather's already lost his house. Hmm ... Old people are so careless about their own safety.'

Svend didn't tell you that Julius was under threat.

'You'll be pleased with me,' says Svend.

Suddenly, you feel sick. Svend's about to betray you, and you're stuck inside a shed full of explosives.

'Why?' asks Erik.

Turn to page 114

Svend hesitates. Your stomach flips up and down like a dolphin over the waves.

'B ... back there,' he stammers. 'I tied Rigmor and that nosy little ranger to a fir tree. That's why I've got my gun out. See, I've still got the safety catch off.' He holds up his gun.

Erik beams. 'You've done well, my Viking-in-training. Tonight I will grant you full Viking status and you'll truly be one of us.'

Svend looks scared. You wish he would smile. Erik might get suspicious.

Erik rubs his beard. 'I expected enthusiasm.'

'It's hard to take in. It's such an honour.' Svend smiles. 'I am so happy.'

'Good,' says Erik, approvingly. 'Now, will we dispose of the rangers first, or load up the longship with more explosives for the submarine?'

'Definitely dispose of the rangers first,' Svend says quickly.

'Thor's thunder! Feel like a little blood-letting, Svend? You are indeed a worthy Viking.' Erik turns around to his four men. 'Come on. It's time to dispatch the rangers. Do you want to lead the way, Svend?'

Turn to page 115

From page 114

'I need more ammo from the shed,' says Svend. 'I've only got one bullet left.'

Erik roars with laughter. 'Why, you blood-thirsty, greedy boy, Svend. You want to take out both of them?'

Svend nods. 'I'll be along in a moment.'

'Catch up with us. I'll ask a few questions, and then they're all yours.' Erik and his men tramp up the track.

Relief floods through you. And how lucky you and Rigmor crept through the woods to the beach so Erik won't find your footprints on the snowy track.

You and Rigmor slink out of the shed and join Svend on the beach.

'Thanks, Svend.' Rigmor grasps his hand.

'What's this?' shouts Erik. The sun glints on his silver helmet as he thunders, yelling, towards you.

He's terrifying.

'Hurry up!' shouts Rigmor, who jumps into the longship.

The boat rocks gently as you hurtle in.

'Svend!' you scream.

He races up. 'I don't want this gun anymore.'

You watch the gun fly through the air and into the shed. A huge bang like twenty New Year's Eves of fireworks explodes in the air. Your ears ring with the noise. Tall orange, red and yellow flames swallow up the shed.

Turn to page 116

From page 115

'Whoops,' says Svend. 'Forgot the safety catch.'

Rigmor picks up a pair of oars and the longship shoots backwards. 'It's the beauty of the Viking design. The stern, or back of the boat, is very thin and light and just like the front of the boat. Made for fast getaways.'

'Lean forward,' she shouts.

You and Svend crouch over, as a bullet sails into the dragon head on the prow.

'Well done,' says Rigmor. 'They're trapped. I assume they used this boat to reach the park.'

Svend nods. 'Erik pretended to take cultural Viking tours so he could travel in national park waters. There's a special porthole in the boat that the submarine docks into, and supplies can be passed unseen.'

'Next time, tell me,' says Rigmor.

'I thought I should be able to deal with it.'

A thought hits you. 'Erik can use the dogs to escape.'

Rigmor smiles. 'Soon rangers and the police will swarm over the national park. I activated my emergency transmitter. Also, the dogs are very well trained. They become bad-tempered if strangers try to use them.'

Suddenly, you hear ferocious barking, before a wail wafts out into the fjord.

THE END

You should return to Rigmor. She'll be wondering where you are, and your footprints will be covered up by the falling snow.

You turn back and trudge through the snowy forest towards the car park.

Then it hits you. This could be an elaborate trap, and you've walked right into it. Your skin prickles. Whoever wrote the message probably wanted you and Rigmor to follow the footprints. It's only luck that Rigmor isn't with you.

You listen carefully to discover if you're being followed. You watch snowflakes drift silently to the ground.

Hold on. You hear a faint noise. It sounds muffled, but it's definitely getting louder.

117

If you wait to see what is making the noise, turn to page 118
If you run back towards the car park, turn to page 129

Quickly, you hide behind the nearest tree trunk.

You hold your breath and wait.

A Eurasian lynx slinks between the trees.

You breathe out. The lynx won't hurt you, unless you corner and attack it. It's about one hundred centimetres long with a short, stubby tail. You look at the distinctive tufts of black hair at the tips of its ears.

No wonder you could hardly hear its approach. The fur on the bottom of its feet is like a sort of a snowshoe, and insulates the cat from the extremely cold temperatures.

Wait until you tell Rigmor that you were frightened by a small cat ...

You hear a swishing noise, and an arrow flies over your shoulder.

It could be a hunter after the lynx or it could be someone after you.

Turn to page 120

From page 118

You dive behind another tree a bare second before an arrow embeds itself in the trunk.

You're the prey.

Yanking the arrow out, you sprint between the trees looking for shelter. Arrows hail the ground, but you glimpse the car park ahead and keep running.

Finally, you dash out of the forest, down the slope and into the car park. You tramp through the snow towards the red jeep.

'Hey,' says Rigmor.

You look around. Where is she?

You spot her sitting on the snow between two cars, rubbing her head. She has a huge lump on the top of her head.

Turn to page 121

'Someone crept up behind and hit me when I was walking towards the air terminal,' Rigmor says, 'and then the person dragged me here.'

'We'd better get you to a doctor.' You reach down and pull her up.

'I'm fine. But what about you?'

'Someone doesn't like me and fired these.' You hand her the arrow you pulled out of the tree.

She examines the arrow. 'I don't understand. This is a perfect replica of a Viking arrow. See the reddish, stone tip? That's made of icelandite, a type of andesite, which is an extremely hard volcanic rock. This could only have been made in Iceland.'

'We need to find out who did this and why,' you say.

Rigmor smiles. 'Well, Ranger in Danger, how do you feel about cancelling the ice hotel and going to the land of fire and ice?'

'Iceland? We're already at the airport. Let's go!'

Turn to page 122

You stamp your feet on the volcanic rocks to keep warm. Iceland is the windiest place ever.

You glance across the geyser field to Rigmor. Steam shrouds her. Someone left Rigmor a message at the airport to meet here.

A puffin waddles on bright orange, webbed feet towards you. It's so cute, with its triangular shaped eyes, red, yellow and blue parrot beak, and chubby white tummy and cheeks. It flies up into the air and its stumpy black wings beat up to one hundred times per minute to keep it aloft, then it dives into the sea. That's where it's the expert. It can dive to depths of fifteen metres and stay underwater for a minute.

You turn up the collar of your orange jacket. Everywhere stinks of rotten eggs from the sulphur in the steam that shoots out of the fumaroles or openings in the Earth.

'Do you think he's even coming?' you yell, as a geyser shoots water six metres into the air.

Rigmor covers her ears. She can't hear you.

You wander across a series of mud pots, formed by hot water rising to the surface where the soil is volcanic ash or clay. The mud bubbles, sometimes exploding like a baby volcano.

You look down at a body.

Turn to page 124

'Rigmor,' you yell.

She looks across and breaks into a run.

You stare down at the man's body. He's still breathing, although his skin is badly burned. He wears a ranger uniform.

You summon help while Rigmor calms the man. Carefully, you both heave him out of a mud pool. In a normal situation you would leave a burns victim where they are until medical help arrives, but you don't have that option here.

'Rigmor,' he whispers.

She kneels down and spreads her jacket over him to try to stop his body temperature from plummeting. You pillow his head with your scarf.

He murmurs softly. 'A Viking longship found. It's buried. They'll take it out of our country forever. It's in the national park west of here. Erik ... mining company ... but also he's ...' The ranger lapses into unconsciousness.

Ten minutes later, the helicopter arrives, quickly collects the injured man, and leaves.

'Ready?' asks Rigmor.

You nod and sprint to the jeep.

Turn to page 125

From page 124

Rigmor stops the jeep at the top of a mountain. 'Here's the national park.'

It's the weirdest place you've ever seen. A glacier carves the park in half. One side is lush grass with scattered patches of wildflowers – blue, pink and yellow. On the other side, a volcano belches smoke, and glowing red lava fields surround it. There's also a huge area of barren, greyish rocky land. 'It looks like a moonscape,' you say.

'Bingo,' says Rigmor. 'Members of the Apollo missions, including Neil Armstrong, trained there to walk on the Moon.'

You gaze out at sea. 'What's that?'

Rigmor pulls her binoculars up to her eyes. 'I don't believe what I'm seeing. You check it out.'

You stare through the powerful binoculars. You feel as if you've slipped back hundreds of years in time. 'Is that a Viking ship?'

'We'd better check it out, even if it isn't the buried Viking ship. I haven't heard of any re-enactments going on around here.' Rigmor starts the jeep and you speed off towards the ocean.

She parks the jeep behind a rock. You grab a spade in case you need to dig a shelter or something else.

You creep up to the scrubby bushes lining the shore. A large bird flaps up. Something wet lands on your head.

Turn to page 126

From page 125

You stick your finger into gross, smelly bird vomit.

'That was a fulmar, a type of petrel,' murmurs Rigmor. 'They have a unique feature of vomiting on you if you annoy or scare them.'

To judge by the amount of vomit dripping down your beanie, you both annoyed and scared it.

You train the binoculars on the Viking ship. An elaborately carved dragon head decorates the fore post, the pointed structure that curves up the ship's bow.

The ship slides onto the beach. A tall man with a fur cape and a horned silver helmet leaps onto the gritty black sand. He gazes towards you.

'Thor's thunder! We're being watched – or that's a very strange orange creature with binoculars in the bushes. Capture them, men. They will learn that nobody can interfere with Erik.'

Four men, all wearing horned helmets, jump out of the ship and run towards you. In their hands, they hold gleaming silver swords.

'That must be the Viking who hit me in the car park. And the burnt ranger spoke of an Erik.' Rigmor starts to spring up, but you hold her back.

Turn to page 128

One of the Vikings runs towards the rock where Rigmor hid the jeep. You can't go there now. 'We need to separate,' you say. 'They don't know that there are two of us. I'll get them to chase me. I know I can outrun them; their heavy swords and helmets will slow them down. Meet me up at that huge boulder way over where the glacier lies.'

You sprint off before she argues. It's the only way.

The grass is green and springy under your feet. One thing you do well is run, and your body settles into a steady rhythm. You feel as if you could run for kilometres. Even though you're still carrying the heavy spade, your breathing hardly alters as you charge up a mound.

Splat! You sprawl on the ground with the green and springy grass in your mouth. You wriggle your toes to check nothing's broken. It seems okay. Something dark pokes up out of the grass. That's what tripped you.

You reach over and scrape it with your finger. Wood fibres collect under your nails. This could be the buried Viking longship.

You try to guess how far away Erik and his gang are. Will you have time to have a bit of an exploratory dig?

If you decide not to dig, turn to page 144
If you decide to dig, turn to page 132

No way are you going to stick around to find out what's making that noise. You need to get back to Rigmor and to safety.

You charge through the forest, slipping and sliding in the snow. You don't have time to look where you put your feet; you just need to get out of here quickly.

'Agggghhhhhh!'

You tip upside down as a lasso around your ankle tightens and pulls you upwards. The blood rushes to your head as you dangle helplessly from a rope trap.

'Oh, what have we here?' booms a man's voice.

129

Turn to page 130

From page 129

You slip out your pocketknife and desperately try to saw the rope.

'I'll help you with that,' says the man.

A sword swishes the pocketknife out of your hand. You twirl around on the rope and see a man with long reddish hair and a neatly trimmed beard. He wears a fur cape and a metal helmet with two horns. Does he think he's a Viking?

'You're a strange-looking reindeer,' he says. 'Shame you didn't watch where you put your feet, a young eager ranger like you.'

'Let me down,' you order.

He laughs, sounding exactly like a barking seal. 'Hmmm. Maybe I'll just keep you hanging there.'

'But I'll freeze,' you say.

'It's a pity, isn't it? I'm not sure what to do with you,' says the Viking. 'Yet ...'

THE END

From page 97

Are you crazy? A ranger would never agree to be a double agent. No ranger would ever betray the natural environment.

Go home immediately!

THE END

From page 128

If you dig and find that it is actually the Viking longship, you can take a few photos.

Then you'll have authenticated proof of its existence, and Rigmor will be able to arrange protection.

You thrust the spade into the springy turf. Dirt and grass fly everywhere as you dig like a demented mole. You remember the original Scandinavian name for mole was 'dirt tosser' ...

Suddenly, you shovel air, as the spade meets no resistance. The ground moves below you.

You hurtle downwards.

132

Turn to page 133

From page 132

Ouch! You lie spread-eagled on a scrubbed, pine table.

Two adults and a young boy sit around you with knives and forks in their hands. They looked stunned to find you in the middle of the table.

'This wasn't what I expected for dinner,' murmurs a blonde woman.

'Yuck,' says the boy. 'This is why I'm vegetarian.'

If you weren't winded, and possibly seriously injured, you would tell him off, but instead you rest and wait until your heart stops fluttering like a puffin's wings.

'What just h ... happened?' you stammer. 'Do you live in the Viking longship?' You smile widely so that they will relax and trust you.

133

'Why is this crazy person lying on our table and pulling that funny face, Mummy?' whispers the boy. 'Will it try to bite us with its teeth?'

You stop smiling.

The man slams his fist down on the table and you all jump.

Turn to page 134

'You're obviously an idiot!' he shouts. 'You dug through our grass-covered roof.'

Whoops. You mistook the roof beams for a Viking longship. It's an easy mistake. Once, many houses in Scandinavia had turf roofs, and this particular house must be built into the side of the hill. Once you explain ...

'You didn't realise that on private property you need to ask permission to dig,' he continues.

Double-whoops. You thought it was a national park.

'If you weren't such a nincompoop, you would have found the door to our holiday house mere metres away.'

You lift up your hand in a 'stop' gesture.

The man stares at the knotted string bracelet on your arm. 'You're one of us?'

He pulls up his jumper sleeve and you see the green-string bracelet with three knots worn by those who support the aims of international rangers.

Bang! Bang! Bang!

'Quick, hide,' says the woman, 'before they break down the door.'

Desperately, you check out the room. A large wooden chest lies beside the wood stove, but that's too obvious a hiding place. There's a silver-grey polar bearskin rug, or maybe you can hide under the table.

If you choose to lie under the polar bear rug, turn to page 136
If you dive under the table, turn to page 143

Maybe if you try to keep your arms rammed against your sides, you'll be a more aerodynamic shape, like a toboggan, and skim through the snow and ice.

You drop the long branch and brace yourself, trying to keep as straight as a snowboard.

More and more snow packs down on you, until you're drowning in it. You suck in a deep breath, but swallow more snow and ice. You try to cough it up. It's useless. The snow suffocates you. It's everywhere.

A memory flashes in your brain about how you should try to swim when caught in an avalanche. Dread fills you as you realise that you've left it too late.

Finally, the avalanche stops, but you're buried deep under it. You know that as soon as an avalanche stops, the snow and ice set like concrete. A tiny part of your brain marvels that it really does feel as if you're encased in head-to-toe plaster.

135

You should have tried to hold up your branch and then Rigmor might know where to find you. Now all she'll see is tonnes of snow, ice, rocks and branches.

You yell and scream, but you can't hear yourself properly because snow blocks your ears. You can hardly keep your eyes open you're so tired. You'll worry about being rescued after you've had a little nap ...

THE END

From page 134

You crawl under the polar bear rug that's black underneath. Black absorbs heat from the Sun, so black skin helps the polar bears keep warm. The skull is big enough for you to slide your head inside and look through the bear's glass eyes.

You hear the door fling open.

'I'm Erik, the last of the true Vikings.'

Fear surges through you, but you lie still. If Erik spies the bearskin shaking he'll be suspicious.

'You nearly broke down my door,' says the man, angrily. 'I'm phoning the police.'

'You don't want to do that,' says Erik. 'We'll have a quick look around, then forget we were ever here.'

You hear a creak, and the slam of the chest.

'Did you hunt that polar bear yourself?' asks Erik. 'It's a huge specimen. Must be three metres.'

'It was on an ice floe near our beach. More and more polar bears will reach Iceland as pieces of ice break off the Arctic pack due to global warming.'

It seems weird a conservationist and supporter of the environment hunts polar bears, but hunting is part of Scandinavian culture.

Suddenly, Erik's boots fill your vision.

Turn to page 137

'Have you seen a ranger in a bright orange jumper and jacket, about so high?' asks Erik. 'No? That's strange. The hole in your roof looks as if someone dropped in.'

You reach forward and yank Erik's legs. He topples over backwards, and you leap up and dash towards the still-open door.

You pull the polar bearskin tightly around you and head for the shelter of some bushes up on the next ridge. It's hard to see through the bear's glass eyes, but you figure the silver-grey bearskin will camouflage you more than your bright orange jumper and jacket.

The landscape changes from springy grass to the hard, grey rock surface of the moonscape. The silver grey of the polar bearskin will blend in well here.

You sprint as fast as you can. Polar bears can speed up to forty kilometres per hour on land for short distances. You're not that fast, but you're doing okay. Soon you reach some scrappy greyish bushes and collapse panting, on the hard, rocky surface. Gradually you stop wanting to throw up. Time to check out Erik and his gang.

You crouch over and peer through the bushes.

'Ow!' Pain floods through your body.

You look behind. A smiling couple in hunting gear approach you. You fling off the bearskin.

Their jaws drop, and they race towards you.

The sleeve of your bright orange jacket turns red.

137

Turn to page 138

The couple visit you later, after you wake up in hospital.

'We're so sorry,' says the woman, 'but we thought ...'

'... I was a polar bear,' you finish.

'It was a reasonable mistake,' says Rigmor, beside you.

'That polar ... best piece of shooting I ever did.' The man from the turf house lies in a bed next to you.

'Why are you here?' you ask.

'Why didn't you trust me to help you when you were in my house? Then you wouldn't be here. My name's Berg, by the way, and this is my wife, Kristin, and my son, Galdur.'

'Hey,' you say. 'Did Erik and his thugs hurt you?'

Your throat tightens. It would be your fault.

'Berg helped us capture them,' says Rigmor. 'Erik owns a mining company responsible for incredible environmental damage throughout Scandinavia. Since his arrest, the shares in his company have plummeted. He'll be bankrupt. Kristin has been a great help.'

Kristin smiles. 'I own several Scandinavian newspapers. I told people the truth. Erik's illegal mining exploration in a submarine interferes with the sonar system of whales and causes them to beach on land. His oil spills kill seals, dolphins and other marine life. Pure rivers silt up from his mines, resulting in the loss of fish. Erik is a total environmental vandal.'

Turn to page 139

'But, Berg, why are you here?'

'After you raced off, I locked the door. No way would I let those scoundrels catch you. Kristin and Galdur, you were a very good lad Galdur, let off flares through the hole in the roof. Soon help arrived and that horned, helmeted fool and his little men were arrested.'

'Did they beat you up?' You stare at Berg anxiously, but he looks fine.

'No. Kristin did a bit of whacking with our cast-iron fry pan, didn't you?'

'It made such a satisfying clang against those silly steel helmets,' she says.

'Due to the well-built nature of our cottage, it was impossible for them to escape except via your entry point hole in the roof or through the locked door.'

'But didn't they force you to give them the key?'

'It was a bit hard to get the key,' says Kristin.

'I swallowed it,' says Berg. 'I know it was a stupid thing to do, and I won't ever do it again, but I panicked. We're part of one family, trying to preserve nature. I'm to stay in hospital until it comes out the other end. You can have the cleaned key as a souvenir.'

'Maybe not,' you say hastily.

The whole room explodes into laughter.

THE END

'I need to get my balance,' you say. 'It makes me queasy to jump over water. I can hardly walk along a pier if I glimpse any water through the cracks.'

'Move,' orders Erik.

'I need a moment,' you say. 'Svend, go next.'

Svend looks at Erik, who nods.

The dinghy rocks as Svend jumps across to the submarine.

Now the four men who rowed the boat remain. They're too big for you to get past. You'll have to try to trick them. You know that when a submarine dives, the top vents are open so that when the water floods into the outer ballast tanks, all the air is driven out through the vents. Can you use this somehow?

'Look, down there!' You point to the water between the dinghy and the submarine.

They peer over the side of the dinghy.

You rush to the other side, fling off your heavy fur coat and lob it into one of the air vents. Then you leap into the sea, scooping up as many oars as you can.

It's gaspingly cold. You sink, and swallow a huge gulp of seawater.

Turn to page 141

From page 140

You surface and suck in fresh air. You've got five out of a possible eight oars. That should slow down Erik and his crew.

You need to try to keep as much of your body as possible out of the icy water. If you stay still, you use up less of your body's heat, but you don't have that choice. You need to swim to shore.

You heave your body partially onto the oars and start kicking. At least your head and face are out of the freezing water.

'Find the ranger!' shouts Erik.

Somewhere behind, you hear the sound of oars dipping in and out of the water.

A light flickers on shore, and then another. You speed on, although your feet burn from the cold.

Suddenly, a searchlight floods the sea. You stop and wave an oar in the air.

'Hey,' shouts a voice. It's Rigmor.

'I'm here!' you scream. 'They're in a sub.'

A motor boat putters towards you, and strong arms haul you aboard.

Turn to page 142

From page 141

'Wait,' you say and search the sea behind you. There's no sign of the dinghy, but you glimpse the submarine in the black waters.

Someone takes your pulse, while blankets are wrapped around you.

'Ri ... g ... a,' you start, but you stop because you're slurring your words and it comes out all wrong. You try to speak again, but you can't remember what you wanted to say. Slowly, you sink into darkness.

You wake up in hospital, an electric blanket warming you. An IV drip pumps fluid into your arm. Ironically, hypothermia caused by icy water can cause dehydration, which is the loss of fluid and salts from the body.

Rigmor peeks in the doorway. 'Awake at last, sleeping beauty. You solved the mystery of the blue whales beaching. And Erik will no longer be able to plunder our natural environment.'

'You caught them?'

Rigmor laughs. 'The submarine was unable to dive, and subs are much slower on the surface because they're primarily designed to be underwater. So we arranged for them to be picked up before they fled to the safety of international waters. How did you do that?'

'It was a long shot. I tossed my fur coat over the vents, hoping some of it would block them. It was a total fluke that it worked. You would think a hunter like Erik would have spotted a fake fox.'

THE END

From page 134

You dive under the table and wait.

You hear footsteps walk across the wooden floor. The door creaks open, then the room fills with shouting, stamping men.

'Quiet!' screams a voice. 'I am Erik, the last of the Vikings.'

'Please leave my home right now,' says the woman's voice.

'As soon as we search it. Men, you check out the rooms off the passage.'

Footsteps race along the wooden floor.

'Little boy,' says Erik. The toes of his boots poke under the table. 'Is someone hiding here?'

You hold your breath. Your heart beats so loudly you think Erik will hear it.

'Why has the funny man got horns sticking out of his head, Mummy? Does he want to look like a cow?'

You relax.

'No-one along here,' calls out a voice, and the room fills with the stamping of boots again.

'We'll be off then,' says Erik. 'Sorry to bother you. I advise you to forget we were here.'

The front door slams.

143

Turn to page 146

A part of you longs to dig, but now is the wrong time, with Erik and his gang chasing you. Also, Rigmor expects to meet up at the big boulder near the glacier. You run onwards.

When you reach the boulder, there's no sign of Rigmor. She could be hiding.

'Rigmor,' you whisper

'Here.'

You sprint towards her voice and fall flat on your face, yet again. You bang your hand on a rectangular stone with strange markings.

'Hey, Rigmor. I've found a rune.'

She runs out and squats beside you. 'It's very worn, but if I feel the shape of the letters I might decipher what it says.'

With her fingertips, she touches the markings. 'Here lies Blue Beard Long Shanks.'

Her eyes widen until they're huge. 'He was a famous Viking. It's rumoured that when he died they buried him in his longship with all his treasures and his dog.'

'Bit unfair to the dog,' you say.

'I agree,' says Rigmor, 'but that's what Vikings did. Blue Beard Long Shanks was said to be the richest man in the world. When a rich Viking died, sometimes he requested to be buried with his longship and his belongings so he could take them into the next world.'

Turn to page 147

From page 143

'I'll leave now.' You climb out from under the table. 'Thanks for everything.'

'Stay,' says the man. 'I'm ringing the police.'

'I need to continue my mission. I'll return soon, and then I'll tell you the whole story.'

You edge the door open. No sign of anyone.

You take a deep breath and dash through the door.

A rope tightens around your waist. You've been lassoed from above.

Erik hauls you up to the roof. 'Thor's thunder, did you think I was a fool and thought the hole in the roof was some sort of skylight? The dirt on the floor was a giveaway of what happened.'

146

You struggle, but it's hopeless. One of the men tosses you over his shoulder like a sack of turnips.

'You won't have the chance to interfere with me again,' says Erik.

THE END

From page 144

'Maybe his ship and treasure is nearby,' you suggest.

Rigmor nods. 'But it's said that bad things befall those who meddle with a burial ground.'

'Couldn't we check it out?' you ask.

'Yes, couldn't we all check it out?' says a voice.

You turn around and see Erik and his men beside the boulder.

'Your orange outfit makes it very easy to find you. You've got a spade. Dig,' orders Erik.

You look at Rigmor who nods, so you lean over and dig. You can't resist flinging one spadeful of soil in Erik's direction. It showers his men.

'I'll do it,' says one, grabbing the spade. You notice dirt in his beard. Good!

He digs furiously. Suddenly, he disappears. You all tiptoe over to the hole.

The man sits in a huge chamber, rubbing the back of his head.

'It's amazing,' whispers Rigmor.

You all stare at the perfect, oak Viking longship. A fearsome-looking monster or gargoyle is carved into the fore post on the bow of the ship.

'This will be the discovery of the decade,' says Rigmor.

'Of the century,' says Erik. 'And I won't let you steal it.'

He thrusts you and Rigmor into the hole.

Turn to page 148

147

You land with a thump on the hard dirt.

Rigmor springs up with her hands on her hips. 'What do you mean *you* won't let us steal it? You're the one who wants to steal it.'

'Are you mad?' yells Erik. 'I'm a Viking. I preserve all Viking heritage. This longship belongs here and here alone. I heard rumours that someone planned to find and steal it. Then when we arrived, you were spying on us.'

Rigmor laughs. 'That's because we're rangers. We suspected you of being up to no good. We found a ranger in a boiling mud pool who spoke of you.'

'Not Frimann?' asks Erik. 'He told me of his suspicions, and we became friends. He's going to become an adviser for my mining company. He convinced me that, as a Viking, I should care for all nature. We planned to work together to create solutions to any environmental problems caused by my company.'

'It's true that he didn't accuse Erik,' you say.

'But,' says Rigmor, 'yesterday, you hit me in the car park in Norway.'

'I was at a meeting here in Iceland yesterday,' says Erik.

'It could be anyone wearing a helmet with horns, Rigmor,' you mutter.

'Quite right,' says a voice.

Erik and the rest of his men tumble into the hole.

Turn to page 149

From page 148

A man dressed as a Viking appears at the edge of the pit. A woman dressed in furs stands beside him.

'Thank you for locating this site. I've searched for years. You lot can stay here, until I get my work crew to haul out the boat.'

'It's a ship,' cries Erik.

'If I may continue?' the man says. 'Actually, none of you can stop me. This *boat* will sell for millions.'

'But why did you try to warn me away at the airport?' you ask.

'All part of my plan. Rigmor is famous throughout Scandinavia as one of the cleverest rangers that ever roamed a national park, and you are the famous, or rather infamous, Ranger in Danger. I thought if I lured you both to Iceland that you two would be the ones most likely to uncover where Blue Beard Long Shanks, or, as I prefer to call him BBLS, was buried. I had a whole series of clues to set you off on the chase, but you've already found it. Thank you for that. Goodbye.'

'Who are you?' yells Erik.

'A soon-to-be very rich gentleman.'

'And his wife,' says the woman.

They disappear, and a car starts up and drives away.

Turn to page 150

149

'What now?' asks Erik.

'Let's move the Viking longship?' you suggest.

Erik looks shocked. 'It can't be damaged.'

'We'll be careful,' says Rigmor. 'Come on.'

Carefully, you push the ship until the carved gargoyle head rests just below the edge of the hole.

Two minutes later, you, Rigmor and Erik stand at the top.

'We'll catch him when he returns,' Rigmor says.

'We need to hide first.' You look around and realise there are hardly any trees in Iceland.

'What about the boulder?' says Rigmor.

You all huddle behind it.

'Now we wait,' says Erik. 'Young ranger, do you know what to do if you're lost in the woods in Iceland?'

That's an easy question. 'You shouldn't move, but wait to be rescued.'

'Normally that's correct,' says Erik, 'but in Iceland if you get lost in the woods, all you need to do is stand up, due to the low stature of our plants.'

Everyone groans.

'Here's another,' says Erik. 'Have you heard …?'

'It's going to be a long wait,' whispers Rigmor.

'But worth it,' you say with a grin.

THE END

From page 87

'Svend, you know this is wrong,' you say, quietly.

He glances from you and Rigmor to the glacier below.

'Svend!' roars Erik.

Svend shakes his head. 'I'm going back to the hotel. It's easier being a waiter than a Viking.'

'Fine,' hisses Erik. He leaps forward and pushes you, Rigmor and Svend all over the precipice, and onto the glacier.

Three screams echo around the glacier. You land with a bump.

Cautiously, you wriggle your toes and move your hands as much as you can inside your giant fur cocoon. Nothing hurts. You survived the fall without any injuries because of the insulation of the fur coat and the reindeer hide. It's unbelievable.

'Check this out,' you say. 'I'm not hurt.'

151

Turn to page 152

From page 151

'Shhhh,' whispers Rigmor. 'It may be to our advantage for Erik not to realise.'

'Are you okay?' you ask.

'I fear my arms are broken, but I am alive. What about you, Svend?'

'My arms are fine, but I can't feel one leg at all. I think it's broken. And the other leg is quite painful.'

'So we have a big ball of fur, me, and with you two, we have two legs and two arms.' It's almost funny. Between them, they make up one working person. You start to laugh but hush immediately as Erik abseils down the steep cliff.

Erik lands on the glacier. He slides out a long sword from under his coat and pulls out a long heavy chain amulet from his pocket and puts it over his head. 'I now wear the chain of retribution or reckoning. You'll all have a proper Viking ending,' he says. 'Who wants to be first?'

He waits as you all lie there in silence.

You look at Svend, who has two working arms, and slowly circle your head. He stares at your huge fur cocoon and nods.

Turn to page 153

'Svend, I wouldn't smile if I were you. Don't expect me to forgive you for your disloyalty. I think you'll be first to go.' Erik takes a step towards Svend.

'No,' says Rigmor. 'Me first. I'm the oldest and a senior ranger. It's only right I should be the first to die.'

'Well, if you insist,' says Erik, turning away from where you and Svend lie closely together. He grips his chain tightly. 'Rigmor, your time has come.'

Svend pushes you with all his might and you roll across the ice, gathering momentum. You smash into the back of Erik's legs.

He sprawls backwards on the glacier and Rigmor leaps onto his chest.

Somehow Erik has managed to impale his sword through his amulet chain, so he lies there choking.

'Stop struggling and you won't choke. We'll undo you in a moment. But this is indeed a true Viking ending,' says Rigmor. 'It really is the chain of reckoning.'

153

THE END

The shape of the man through the blind already seems shadowy. Perhaps you imagined it all. 'Rigmor, maybe we should do the normal patrol, but be watchful.'

Rigmor smiles. 'I agree, but if we spot anything while we're out counting reindeer, we'll be there in a flash. Instead of patrol by plane or pony, we'll ski. It's fast, quiet and fun.'

An hour later, you zoom up and down hills. It feels amazing to be the first person to leave tracks in the snow. A herd of reindeer gallop out of the forest. Quickly, you count them. 'Do you make eighty-four, Rigmor?'

She nods and writes in her notepad. 'Once there were more,' she says, sadly. 'It's harder for the reindeer to find the lichen they graze on, due to human induced climate change. The snow thaws in the increased temperatures, and then re-freezes, making it almost impossible for the animals to dig through the layers.'

You stare at the reindeer. 'I heard more than 400 reindeer drowned in Sweden when the thin layer of ice on a river cracked when the reindeer were herded across.'

'Yes,' says Rigmor. 'For many generations, herders took that path, but suddenly, the ice was no longer as thick. And people say climate change doesn't exist ...'

The crack of a rifle rings out. The reindeer herd swings around like a wave and flees into the nearby fir forest.

Rigmor stares across at a nearby hill. 'Look.'

Turn to page 155

A tall man armed with a rifle is about a kilometre away. There are four other men with him.

A wolverine crouches metres away from them.

'Why doesn't it run away?' you ask. Wolverines are speedy, and usually keep well away from humans.

'It must be trapped,' says Rigmor.

The tall man lifts up the rifle and aims directly at the dark-brown wolverine.

'Stop!' screams Rigmor.

The man glances across, then turns back to the wolverine. He lines up his gun.

Rigmor grabs her rifle from her backpack and shoots.

The tall man drops his gun, and hugs his hand.

'Bullseye,' you whisper, as you follow Rigmor down the slope towards the men.

When you reach them, the four men stare at Rigmor in awe. The tall man hunches over on the ground.

You ski across to the wolverine. A trap encases one large, furry paw. The wolverine snarls, but you can tell it is tiring. You break off a twig and press the trap's release lever down. The wolverine scampers up a nearby fir tree.

'Where is your permit to kill a wolverine?' asks Rigmor in a calm voice. 'I know none have been issued recently in this park. The wolverine is an endangered animal and can only be shot if you have a permit.'

Turn to page 156

Rigmor steps back as the tall man leaps up. He looks a little like a wolverine himself, with his heavy build, dark brown hair and huge snarl. 'It's a wolverine. Don't you know that they're the devil incarnate?'

Rigmor laughs. 'Are you mad? That is nothing but superstition. The wolverine is the largest member of the weasel family, and it is no more evil than you or I.'

The tall man growls. 'Well, you hurt me, you fix me up,' he says, holding out his dripping hand. The bullet passed through the fleshy part below his thumb.

You pull out the first aid kit, while Rigmor radioes for backup.

'Men, seize them!' shouts the tall man.

The four men stand still. 'Sorry, Erik,' says one. 'This ranger shot you with one shot from a kilometre away.'

Did he say Erik? You dart over and pull open the tall man's backpack. A horned Viking helmet sits at the top. 'Paid me an early morning visit?' you ask.

Erik slumps on the ground. 'Surrounded by fools and rangers. There is no fate worse on this Earth.'

'I wouldn't say that,' says Rigmor. 'I think things will get worse and worse for you, once we investigate.'

Something cracks above you. A waterfall of wolverine wee splashes down on Erik.

Talk about a stench. 'Revenge of the wolverine. You're no longer Erik the Viking, but Erik the Stinking.'

THE END

GLOSSARY

Avalanche A large amount of snow sliding rapidly down a slope. It gains speed and power as it moves, burying or sweeping away anything in its path.

Ballast Heavy material to stabilise a ship or plane.

Blubber An insulating layer of fat under the skin of whales and other large marine mammals.

Bow Front part of a boat.

Fjord A long narrow inlet of sea between steep cliffs.

Geyser A natural hot spring that periodically erupts, throwing steam and hot water into the air.

Glacier Slowly moving river of ice.

GPS unit Global positioning system.

Hart Male deer.

Hull The frame or body of a ship.

Husky A type of dog, often used to pull sleds. Their noses dry up at night so they don't freeze up in subzero temperatures.

Kraken Mythical many-armed sea monsters that lived off the coast of Scandinavia. When the Kraken attacked a ship, it wrapped its arms around the hull capsizing it, and then ate the crew.

Lichen A number of complex plant-like organisms made up of an alga and a fungus growing together. The fungus protects the alga, and the alga provides the fuel needed for the two organisms to survive. A sample of lichen was sent up in a spaceship and directly exposed to outer space for 14.6 days. Despite the vacuum of space, cosmic radiation and intense temperatures, the lichen survived.

Mine   Bomb planted in the ground or in water.

Periscope   An optical instrument that, in its most basic form, consists of a long tube with parallel mirrors at each end, inclined at 45 degrees to its axis. Usually associated with submarines, soldiers used it for secret observation in the trenches during World War I.

Runes   The Viking system of writing on stone, wood or bone. The basic alphabet had 16 letters. Bills, accounts and love messages were written in runes on sticks.

Sonar   Sound Navigation and Ranging. Active sonar emits pulses of soundwaves that travel through the water, reflect off objects, and return to the receiver on the ship. Used for navigation.

Thor   Norse god of thunder, war and strength.

Viking   Scandinavian sea-borne raiders in the Middle Ages. Much of the year they were farmers and fisherman, but during the summer they followed their local leader across the seas to other countries to trade and raid.

Viking longship The oak ship had a long narrow hull and a shallow keel so it was fast and could sail onto beaches. The Vikings could jump out, raid, and then make a quick getaway.

The Real
Rigmor

Rigmor Solem is Chief Ranger at Norway's Jotunheimen National Park. Since she was young, Rigmor dreamed of working in the forest. She attended university and began work as a seasonal ranger where she soon discovered her real passion was for mountains. Now she could never live anywhere without mountains.

She lives close to a national park amongst the mountains with her husband, two horses, one dog and one cat. She also has an 18-year-old daughter.

Rigmor, really, is an amazing shot with a rifle.

The Thin Green Line
FOUNDATION

Using profits from his film, *The Thin Green Line*, which has been shown in more than fifty countries, and from donations received from people all over the world, Sean Willmore started The Thin Green Line Foundation.

The Thin Green Line looks after the welfare of rangers' families where the ranger has been killed in the line of duty, and supports community conservation projects to prevent ranger deaths and protect wildlife.

To find out more about The Thin Green Line, or to support their work on the frontline of conservation, check out www.thingreenline.org.au

You can join the rangers on The Thin Green Line by becoming a member, purchasing their Power of One pack (includes a DVD of the film *The Thin Green Line*, an eco T-shirt, sticker, calico bag and membership), or simply donate to support their valuable work.

It's up to you now!

www.thingreenline.org.au

About the Authors

Sean Willmore worked as a ranger on Victoria's Mornington Peninsula, until he found out that rangers around the world were being routinely killed and injured in the course of their duties and felt compelled to do something. He sold his car, remortgaged his house, and took off around the world with his camera. The result was his documentary *The Thin Green Line*, and the foundation of the same name. His efforts to bring attention to, and support, the dangerous work undertaken by these conservation heroes, have won him international acclaim.

Alison Reynolds (www.alisonreynolds.com.au) lives in suburban Melbourne, but she often feels she is a ranger in danger. She has a pack of wild dogs, possums tapdance on the roof all night, and the neighbour's scarily giant rabbits bounce across the front yard. Then there are the cats, bats and marsupial rats. Along with Sean, she loves to choose her own adventures and hopes you do, too!